YOURS

A Dark Bad Boy Romance Novel

By

Aubrey Dark

Check out the complete Aubrey Dark collection:

His

Mine

His Gift
His Ransom
Mr. Black's Proposal

-

Available on Amazon now!

Prologue

Jessica

I'm still dreaming, in that half-asleep moment before dawn, when I feel his hand curl between my legs.

It's dark.

It's always dark when he comes for me.

My eyes open slightly as his hand presses between my thighs, the coil inside of me going tight already, making me moan softly with desire. I blink, my eyelashes fluttering against my cheeks, but it's not light outside yet. The sky is a deep, deep gray, the stars turning invisible one by one.

His other hand wraps around my throat. His grip is tight and controlled. Very controlled. That's one thing I've never seen him do—lose control.

"There are two ways to get rid of a shadow, Jessica."

His voice comes through to me as a low murmur. His voice invades my dreams, drives out the demons. His strong fingers grip my thighs as I twist under him, forcing them apart. I try to move, but my wrists are bound above my head. The rope is cold and tight against my skin.

I open my mouth to cry out, and his lips press down against mine. He seals in my moan as his fingers push into the place where I am already slick. When he breaks apart from the kiss, I can only gasp his name.

"Vale…"

"The first way is you light a candle. Light hundreds of candles. Put them on the floor, on the shelves, all around you. Light up the whole room with a thousand different pinpoints of light. Your shadow will disappear, right? The brightness swallows it all up."

There is no moon, and the last stars in the sky are too far away, too dim to be candles. I try to move, but my wrists are bound above my head. Is this a dream? I have been dreaming this dream for my whole life, maybe.

His mouth is on my neck, and his hand strokes me where I am now dripping wet with desire. If I had panties on, they would be soaked, but I am naked, completely naked. The stars are fading into the fabric of the sky. He moves down, farther, farther.

"Vale—"

He pins my hips with his strong hands, and his tongue sinks into me. He thrusts me from one dream into another, with no time to wake. Then he releases me, and I arch up in agony, needing to be satisfied.

"Two ways to get rid of a shadow," he says again, and now the sky is pale and thin and all the stars have disappeared, but the rope is still around my wrists and I am still aching for his touch.

"The second way is easy," he says, and the coil inside me winds tighter. When he speaks, his breath sends shivers across my sensitive skin, shivers that deepen and resonate until my whole body is vibrating for him.

"*Vale.*" My voice is ragged, gasping with desire. His hand comes down and caresses my body slowly, possessively.

YOURS

How? How do I get rid of this shadow? But he answers me before I can speak again.

"All you have to do… is close your eyes."

Chapter One

Vale

"I don't know," Dan said.

This is the best job, I'm telling you. Tell him, Vale."

I leaned over the checkerboard table in the old Hollywood diner and clasped my hands together in front of my brunch plate. Dan squirmed in his seat, like he thought I was going to stab him with my fork. Of course, I wasn't. I would never get blood on a perfectly-cooked omelet.

"It is absolutely the best job," I said. "You get to do what you like, when you like. You control everything."

"But… but you have to _kill people_," he said, whispering the last two words.

Rien laughed. I leaned over my plate toward Dan, pointing in the air with my fork for emphasis. He followed the tines with rapt attention.

"Dan, you _get_ to kill them. They're the bad guys."

Dan rubbed his lips, looking doubtful. Our waitress came by to fill up our coffee cups, and we all clammed up. I eased myself back in my chair.

"Thanks, darling," Rien said to the waitress. "Could I have another stack of pancakes? I'd hate for all this whipped cream to go to waste."

"For you, honey, anything," she said, smiling back at him as she poured his coffee. All of us watched her swishing hips as she walked away from our table, waiting for her to be gone so that we could speak openly again.

She thought we worked for the government. And in a way, we kinda did. The CIA sent their targets to me, and I sent them to Rien to cut up into little bitty pieces. Sometimes, if the targets didn't go for the "federal witness" trap the CIA laid for them, I handled them with a gun. But that was messier.

Rien didn't like messy; he was a clean surgeon. Neither did Dan—he was some forensic tech guy who worked for the local cops. Rien must have had something on him, or I don't think Dan would ever have helped us out. He was too scared for that. He hated blood, and dead bodies, and killing in general.

But he *loved* our stories.

"Alright," I said, "You'll never beat this one. I was hired to kill this guy in Thailand, right? Feds gave me three hundred thousand dollars for the job."

"Who was the target?" Rien asked.

"Some drug lord who got off scot-free after tattling on his associates," I said, chewing a bite slowly. Mmmm. Ham and green peppers. You can't beat a good Denver omelet.

"Why did they want to kill him?"

"This guy… well, this guy was stupid. Sloppy as hell, breaking the borders whenever he wants to fly out to Amsterdam for a joint, hiring underage hookers, gambling with the local chao pho."

"What's that?" Dan asked.

I took another bite of omelet and chewed as I explained.

"That's like the mafia."

"Mafia?"

"The Thai mafia. He's betting around in mob circles,

spreading cash around for cockfights, dogfights, whatever."

"Basically doing all kinds of things you're not supposed to do if you're in the witness protection program," Rien interjected.

"Exactly. So he has this whorehouse he likes to go to, and he always calls ahead to reserve the same ladyboy whore."

"Chicks with dicks?" Dan's eyes were huge. "Oh, man, what a country."

"What, you think we don't got that in America?" I asked, raising my eyebrow.

"Ladyboys? No way."

"Hell yeah, ladyboys. Thai ladyboys, Mexican horsefuckers, Chinese masseuse blowshops. We got everything in America. We're the melting pot of kinky stuff," I said.

"We don't have the crazy shit they have in Japan," Rien said, shaking his head. He swiped his finger through the top of the bowl of whipped cream and licked it off suggestively.

"That's different, man. Japan is, like, the fucking cutting edge of sexual kink technology. They have artificially cultivated watermelons that grow in a plastic mold shaped like an anus. They're cloning half-rabbits, half-women to make real life playboys."

"Are you for real?" Dan asked.

"I don't know, I heard it."

"What, you want to move to Japan?" Rien teased the younger man.

"No!"

"Fuck a watermelon asshole, maybe?"

"*No!*"

I turned back to Dan and waved my fork to get his attention back to my story.

"Anyway, so this ladyboy, I'm trying to offer her a bribe to make things go easy. She doesn't speak English too good."

"Neither do you, huh, Vale?" Rien grinned.

"Fuck off," I said. "So I'm trying to tell her what I'm gonna do, you know."

"You're telling her you're gonna kill the guy?" Dan asked.

"Yeah. I don't want her to freak out when I bust in the room and cut this guy's throat. I'm doing all kinds of, you know, hand gestures, like we're playing charades. Finger across my throat, making dead guy noises, you know."

"Ugh, you had to cut his throat?" Dan looked a bit green.

The waitress came by and slid a plate of pancakes off onto the table on her way to the back of the diner. Rien licked his lips and poured syrup on top.

"You're such a goddamn pussy, Dan. You could never be a killer," I said.

"Not if I'm gonna have to cut anyone's throat, I couldn't!" Dan said, rubbing his neck.

"My girlfriend cut a guy's throat once," Rien said.

"Your girlfriend has bigger balls than Dan," I said.

Dan frowned in confusion at Rien.

"Is your girlfriend a ladyboy?"

"Swear to God, Dan, I'll cut your throat right now," Rien warned. He lifted his butter knife in a threatening gesture.

8

Dan swallowed and turned back to me to hear the rest of the story.

"Anyway," I said, "So I finish gesturing to this whore, and it seems like she gets it. I hand her a hundred bucks in baht, and I make a shushing gesture."

I put my finger to my lips in case Dan didn't get it.

"Like, *shhh* don't tell anyone. And she repeats it, nodding the whole time. So I think we're good."

I paused for dramatic effect.

"Did you fuck her?" Dan blurted out.

"Wh—What? Fuck her? What does that have to do with the goddamn story, anyway? And no, I didn't fuck her. Jesus, Dan. She's a goddamn ladyboy."

"I thought that was the point of the story," Dan said.

"Stop interrupting and we'll get there. So I wait in the back until the mark arrives, and then I give him five minutes more to take off his pants and get busy. Five minutes, and then I come bursting through the door, my knife in the air, ready to slice this guy open. And what do I see?"

Dan shook his head.

"What?"

"The guy is lying on the bed, dead as roadkill. His leg is still gushing blood from the femoral artery."

Dan's jaw dropped halfway down his face. I didn't think he'd eaten a single bite of his brunch. Oh well, his loss. I continued my story.

"The ladyboy comes out of the bathroom. She's totally naked, dick flopping around in front of her, blood on her tits. She's drying the knife off. I stare at the body, then up at her, then back at the body. She smiles and winks, and puts her finger to her lips. '*Shhh*,' she says."

I look at the two men sitting across the table from me and wait for their reaction.

"*Shhh,*" I repeat. "Can you fucking believe it?"

"Holy shit." Dan looked like he was going to throw up.

"Talk about government inefficiencies. They're talking to the wrong vendors." Rien said. He forked a bite of pancake into his mouth.

I dropped my fork onto my plate.

"That's what you took away from the story, Rien? Government waste?"

"Well, they overpaid you by like, two hundred ninety nine thousand—"

"You boys can't appreciate a good hitman story when you hear one."

"Ugh, cut in the leg," Dan said, rubbing his thigh.

"Want to hear the story about how Vale put a gun to my head?" Rien asked.

"Wh—are you for real?"

I laughed.

"That was your own damn fault, Rien, and you know it."

"Why do you even hang out with this guy?" Dan asked Rien.

"Do you know what it's like to kill a man?" Rien asked, his eyes narrow.

"No."

"Well, there you go. It's hard to find a kindred spirit when you're a killer." He popped the last of the pancake into his mouth.

"Hey now," I said, lifting a hand. "I am not your goddamn kindred spirit."

"Yeah? Tell Dan here about what happened to your last girlfriend."

Jen. I did not want to think about her right now. Fortunately, I didn't have to. My cell phone vibrated in my pocket. I pulled it out.

"Shit." It was headquarters. They only called this number when they needed something done urgently. I sighed.

"I gotta get this," I said. I stood up from the table and pushed my chair in.

"Wait," Dan said. "What happened to your last girlfriend?"

I leaned forward and stole a strawberry from Rien's plate. I looked sideways at Dan with the most menacing glare I could.

"*I killed her,*" I whispered.

Dan's face went pale.

I put the phone to my ear. Behind me, I could hear Dan asking Rien if I was telling the truth.

"I need you at the Los Angeles airport," the voice said. "A man will be waiting outside the first terminal. Follow him."

"When?"

"Right now."

"*Right* now? I'm at brunch. And I have a barber's appointment—"

"Right now. This one's important."

The voice hung up and I looked at my watch. It wasn't even eleven o'clock. I turned back to the table.

"Gotta go," I said to Rien. "Big boys have an assignment."

"Now? You haven't even started your pancakes,"

Rien said.

"Can't. Orders are orders. You want them?" I slid the plate over to Rien, who looked way too fit to be demolishing three short stacks of pancakes.

"This is your idea of control?" Dan asked, incredulous. *"This* is doing what you like, when you like? You just wait for the call to go—" his voice dropped to a hush, "—*to go kill people!"*

"Sure. I like to follow orders," I said.

"I like to kill people," Rien said. "Do what you love, and you'll never work a day in your life, am I right?"

"I am so not cut out for this," Dan said.

"Fine. More bodies for us, huh, Rien?" I slapped them both on the shoulders. Rien grinned.

"You two are fucking psycho," Dan said, shaking his head. "Fucking *psycho.*"

Chapter Two

Jessica

"Guys? Hey guys? We missed the downtown exit."

I pressed my face to the window. The metal and glass dome of the San Diego library disappeared behind the other buildings as we sped down the freeway.

"Hey, Mimi. Guys!"

"Do you think she knows yet?" Mimi asked, ignoring me. She winked at April in the rearview mirror.

"Knows what?" I asked, totally confused. I turned around in the passenger's seat of Mimi's SUV. "What don't I know?"

"Oh, Jessica," April said, reaching forward and patting my shoulder. Next to her, her boyfriend James chuckled.

"Are you serious? Hey! What are you doing? We were supposed to be going to the library."

Mimi raised her head and let out a cackle.

"Our evil plan is working!" she cried.

"Oh man, Jessica, I thought you knew," April said, shaking her head.

"Knew what?" I asked.

"Ha, she even brought her Kindle!" Mimi said, poking me in the side. "Jessica, did anyone ever tell you that the dictionary has your name next to the word _gullible_?"

"What? I was going to check out some ebooks. What's going on?" Panic began to bubble up in my chest.

"Wait. Are you *not* dropping me off at the library?"

Mimi shook her head gleefully.

"Jessica, remember when we told you about having fun and taking a break from studying?"

My heart sank. They didn't mean— No. They couldn't. Mimi and April had been talking about taking a trip to Mexico for weeks now. I'd pleaded out of the adventure, but now... Now...

"No," I said.

"Yes."

"No way."

"Yes way!" James chimed in from the back.

"You're kidnapping me?!" I cried out. Mimi and April burst out into laughter. "Are you for real? You guys? Seriously? You are not for real."

"We are totally for real," Mimi said. She raised both her hands in the air. "Tijuana or bust!"

My heart beat fast. The library dome was already far behind us, and I had a sinking feeling Mimi was serious.

"Mimi," I said slowly. "No. You cannot take me to Mexico."

"Give me one reason why not," she said.

"I have to study!" I had three big exams coming up, and I'd planned on using this week to catch up on the material.

"That is the worst reason ever. It's spring break, Jessica! You gotta do some wild and crazy things when you're still in college. Get out. Lose control. Have fun."

"*Ughhhh.*" I slumped back in my seat. "I don't want to have fun."

"What do you want to do?"

"Right now? I want to read books."

"No! Sheesh, Jessica, you're such a priss!"

Mimi grabbed my Kindle off of my lap and tossed it into the back seat.

"Hey! Give it back!"

"No way, braniac," Mimi said.

I spun in my seat, but James was already picking up the ereader.

"*Kidnapped by the Rogue Prince*? Is this what girls like?"

"Give it back!" I squealed.

"Oh my gosh, are you for real?" April said, grabbing the Kindle away from her boyfriend and scrolling through my reading list. My face turned steaming hot.

"April, don't!"

"You have romance novels on that thing?!" Mimi laughed. I groaned in embarrassment as April kept reading aloud.

"*A Pirate's Captive. Taken by the Bad Boy*. I can't believe you read that kind of stuff!"

I would have leapt back into the back seat if we hadn't been driving on the highway. As it was, I buried my face in my hands. My roommates were never going to let me live this down.

"So that's what Jessica fantasizes about, huh?" James said. He poked me from the back seat. "Hey, if you're into bad boys, I have a friend—"

"Stop! Oh my God, stop! I'm going to die of shame," I mumbled.

"I want to hear all about Jessica's fantasies," Mimi said. "What's your favorite?"

"*Please* stop."

"I would never have guessed you would like this stuff," April said, still scrolling through my Kindle. "I thought you would dream about… like, a nerdy poolboy who sits next to you and reads anatomy textbooks to you all day long."

"*Ohhhhhhhh*," I moaned. "Please stop. Turn around. Take me back home so I can throw myself off a roof."

"Don't worry, Jessica," Mimi said, patting me on the back. "As soon as we get a couple of margaritas into you, you'll be *just fine*."

My phone rang. I looked down at the screen.

"Oh, holy God," I said, the blood draining from my face.

"What?" April poked her head into the front of the car.

"It's my mom."

"Uh oh."

"So what?" Mimi asked.

"Jessica's mom is insane," April said.

"She's not insane," I said, feeling weird for defending her. "She's just a little overbearing."

"She called you every morning during midterms to make sure you wouldn't be late for a single test."

"She's protective!"

The phone kept buzzing in my hand.

"Aren't you going to answer it?"

"There's no way I can tell her I'm going to Mexico. She'll flip her lid!"

"Here, gimme."

Mimi plucked the phone out of my hand.

"Mimi! Stop!" I yelped and strained against my seatbelt to try and grab my phone back. Mimi leaned over to the window and answered it.

"Hello?" She held up her hand to shush me. I

shushed, if only to get one of her hands back on the steering wheel.

"Hi Mrs. Quoyle. No, this is Mimi. One of Jessica's roommates?"

I was dying inside, gripping my knees so that I wouldn't be tempted to open the door and throw myself into traffic. My mom would kill me if she knew I was going on a trip and I hadn't told her about it. Mimi grinned at me, driving with her fingernails tapping on the wheel.

"Yes, I understand. She's very busy with her studies and she asked me to take her cell phone away so that she wouldn't be distracted. If it's an emergency, I can tell her—"

In the back, April and James were cracking up with stifled laughter. I glared back at them.

"No? Okay. Would you like me to tell her to call you back? She's studying for the rest of the day, but she should be back from the library before midnight."

April snorted, and James smacked her on the shoulder to shut her up.

"Great. Thanks, Mrs. Quoyle!"

Mimi hung up the phone and tossed it back into my lap.

"What did she say?" I said.

"She said that she's very proud of you for avoiding distractions while you study," Mimi said, a mock serious look on her face.

"You lied to her," I said, staring down at the phone.

"Well, duh."

"You... you lied to her." I had to admit that I had never before considered lying to my mom.

"What did you want me to do, tell her we were going

to Tijuana to slam down as many margaritas as we could?"

"I... no... but what if something happens? She'll go crazy if she doesn't know where I am!"

In the back, April was hooting laughter.

"*Where you are?*" Mimi said. "You're in the library. You're studying for your tests. Just like you wanted to be. Or did you want me to call her back and tell her you're busy reading *Tied up by the Rogue Duke*?" She had an evil glint in her eye, and I didn't doubt for a second she would do it.

"No! But—"

"Come on, Jess," April said. "We'll be back in a couple of days. You can call her tomorrow if you really want to."

"Okay," I said, sighing and staring down at my phone. It felt like I was doing something very, very wrong. But then again, that was supposed to be half the fun.

Right?

Chapter Three

Vale

I walked into the Los Angeles airport behind a young guy in a suit. He looked more nervous than Dan always looked when we talked about killing people. I wondered if Ten had told him about me.

The suit led me through the airport and past one of the security doors into a small office. There were two chairs and a dingy desk.

This is where Ten would meet me? _Figures_.

"Wait here," the nervous guy said. He left me in the office and locked the door behind me.

"I hate waiting," I said to nobody in particular. I took a few paces back and forth before the walls of the office grew boring. God, Ten was something else. Making me come here in the middle of brunch to wait for his sorry ass? This had better be a good mission.

I sat down in the chair and fished into my pocket. Half a joint left. I lit up just as I heard the door opening behind me. Ten walked in, grimacing at the cloud of smoke I blew toward the ceiling.

"Is that pot?" Ten asked.

"Might be."

Ten sat behind the desk. He'd gotten stronger since the last time I'd seen him, and he'd cut his unruly mop of hair. Maybe he'd met a girl.

"Thanks for bringing that in here," he said.

"No problem."

"You know, some of us get randomly drug tested at our jobs."

"Yeah, well, sorry you have a shitty job," I said, taking another drag. The buzz was light. "You shouldn't have made me wait."

Ten frowned, as if deciding whether or not to go after me on this, and then decided it wasn't worth it. He shoved a manila folder across the desk. I picked it up.

"This your new boyfriend?" I asked. The mug shot staring out at me from the file was decidedly one of the ugliest faces I'd ever seen. A bald Mexican dude, maybe forty years old, with a nasty scar running down the left side of his face and a thick black mustache like a bushy caterpillar across his upper lip.

"He's your new boyfriend," Ten said.

"Federal witness?" I scanned down the rest of the file.

"He got off scot-free a year ago. Got sent down to Rosarito to sit pretty. But he's starting to stir up trouble again with the other Mexican druglords."

"Mmm," I said noncommittally.

"We were on the fence with this one. We weren't sure if we'd need him later or not."

"But now?" I looked up at Ten. His face was creased.

"Now, though, there's a body."

"American?"

"American woman, a civilian. Looks like she overdosed on something, washed up on the beach. Someone saw her get into his car at a club."

"Should have sent him to me before you let him escape to Rosarito," I said, closing the file on top of the guy's ugly mug. "I know a plastic surgeon who does wonders with those kinds of assholes."

"Hindsight's twenty-twenty," Ten said, sighing. "He gave us a lot of information on the drug cartels."

"Then you definitely made a mistake."

"How do you know?"

"He's rolling over on the cartels?" I asked, tossing the file back down onto the desk. "Must mean he's involved in something even shadier."

"Maybe."

"So who is this guy? What do I need to know?"

"Alfonze Ensueto, thirty-eight years old. El Alfa, is what he calls himself."

"*The Alpha?* Seriously? Guy sounds like a real tool." I leaned back, rocking the chair on two legs.

"They say he's invincible. That no one can kill him."

"Yeah? So what are you sending me in for?"

"To kill him."

I raised my eyebrows.

"Sounds like an impossible job."

"That's why we're sending you."

"A nice vacation to Baja. You're the best, Ten. What did I ever do to deserve this?"

Ten ignored my sarcasm.

"Don't blow your cover. No matter what. It's your job to get close to this guy, close enough to kill him. Do it right before we raid the estate."

"Which is when?"

"Midnight. The Sunday after next. Try to keep from raising an alarm. Otherwise, we won't be able to get anything from the raid."

"How do you know?"

"We've tried. Twice. The guy's never there; it's just an

empty palace full of armed guards. And nobody knows where he is."

"Maybe he's at church. Have you tried raiding on a weekday instead?"

Ten ignored my joke.

"We'll be able to pull you out during the raid, but you have to kill him first."

"I can do that."

"Alone."

"I heard you the first time," I said.

"Time it as close as you can to the raid itself, or you risk raising the alarm. Vale, we tried this twice."

"You said that already."

"Both times, our man on the inside was killed."

I didn't say anything. Ten didn't like losing men, and I didn't like the idea that I might be dead in two weeks. I clasped my hands together in a pose that was as close to deferential as I could get. Ten continued his speech.

"He's got people around him at all times. His estate in Baja is surrounded by guards. You'll have to be careful."

"Got it. Break in past the guards, get to this guy—"

"You don't need to do that. We've got an in who can get you up close and personal with El Alfa."

I tilted my head. If there was already someone we had working on our side, this should be a piece of cake. I wondered if that's what the other two guys had thought.

"Who is he?" I asked.

"*She* is an escort. Valentina Orizo. El Alfa flies her in from Los Angeles nearly every other week. One of his favorites."

"What's the plan?"

"She'll introduce you to El Alfa as her friend who

needs a job doing anything."

I paused and looked up at Ten. His eyes were dark.

"*Anything?*" I repeated.

"You'll be doing his dirty work, no question about it," Ten said. He didn't meet my eyes.

"And that's okay with you?"

Ten swallowed. I could see his Adam's apple move down his throat, then back up. It was oddly mesmerizing. There must be something he wasn't telling me. This must be bad.

"Your mission is to do whatever needs to be done to get close to him."

I nodded slowly.

"Right."

"You understand me, Vale? *Anything.*"

"This guy's important."

"We think he's behind a few more disappearances than just the one woman. That's what Valentina leads us to believe, anyway. I'm not sure how much she says is true, and how much she says just to get a paycheck from us."

Ten ran a hand through his hair. He looked shaken up. I wondered what other disappearances he was investigating. I wondered if I would be up for the task, if this guy was as unkillable as he thought he was.

"Alright," I said. I stood up and tapped the folder with my fingertips. "When do I get to go after this motherfucker?"

"Right now."

"*Right* now? I need a haircut."

"He's asked for the escort tonight," Ten said. "You fly out in an hour from terminal eighteen. It's a private jet."

"Are you fucking kidding me?" I finished the last drag of my joint and stabbed it out on the top of the desk. Ten winced. "Right fucking now?"

"This is a big deal, Vale."

"How big?"

"A half a million big."

I blew the last of the smoke out between my teeth.

"A half a million? For one guy?"

"Emphasis on the *one*. We don't want to pick up any more bodies than we have to, and you're more likely to get caught if there's a body trail. Don't let anyone see you kill him if you can help it, or you probably won't get out of there at all. Wait until right before the raid, and we'll be there for backup. Can you handle that?"

"Got it. Don't kill anyone. Unless I need to, in which case, do anything."

"Right."

"Thanks for the clear instructions."

"Hey, you're the one who wanted this job. Can you do this?"

"Yeah. Sure, sure. I can do this."

I shook my arms out. Cool. Controlled. I could take down one guy no problem. It was the other stuff—the *anything*—that had me a little concerned.

"Take your time and memorize the file," Ten said.

"Already done." I flipped open the folder once more just to satisfy Ten. El Alfa grimaced out at me.

"You got this under control, Vale?"

"Of course," I said, closing the file and looking up at the man who was sending me across the border to do his dirty work. "I always have things under control."

24

Chapter Four

Jessica

"Mexican Border, 12 Miles." I read the highway sign out loud and sighed. "Tell me this is all a joke."

"No joke," Mimi said.

"What about my passport? I can't go across the border without a passport."

Mimi tapped the dashboard.

"I stole it out of your desk for you. It's right in the glove box."

Ugh. That had been my last hope of convincing them not to take me with them. I let out a deep breath.

"Did you bring a Spanish dictionary?"

"You won't be needing that one bit," April called forward from the back seat. "But you _will_ be needing this."

A clump of red fabric sailed forward and landed in my lap. I picked it up gingerly with my fingertips and held it out in front of me.

"What is this?" I asked.

"It's a dress."

I eyed the skimpy thing. It was a red bandage dress with no sleeves.

"This isn't mine," I said. "I would never have bought this."

"No, it's the one you _should_ have bought when we were out shopping. I picked it up for you, though. So you're welcome."

I looked at the tags. Despite its skimpiness, it said

that it was my size. And then I looked at the price tag. My heart skipped a beat when I realized where the decimal place was.

"I can't afford this dress!" I exclaimed. "Did you see how much it costs?"

"So keep the tag on and don't spill anything on it," April said, shrugging. "We can take it back next week."

"I'll try real hard not to puke margaritas up on you," Mimi said earnestly. "Try it on."

"What do you mean, try it on?"

"I mean put it on."

"Right now? In the car?"

"We're going straight to the club. You can't go out dancing wearing a muumuu that looks like wallpaper from the seventies," Mimi explained, her manicured fingernails tapping the steering wheel impatiently.

"This isn't a muumuu," I said, looking down woefully at my maxi dress. She was right. The print did look like terrible op art.

"Try it on! Try it on!"

April and James joined in the chant.

Try it on! Try it on! Try it on!"

"Ahhh!" I screamed. "Okay, okay, fine!"

"Don't look," I said. "April, cover James' eyes."

"Already closed," James said.

"Better hurry up before we get to the border," April said in a singsong voice.

"Oh, jeez."

I scrambled to pull my so-called muumuu up over my head. I had it off in only a few seconds, but then I fumbled with the red dress.

"Shit," I said. "Which end is down and which end is

up?"

"Are you girls sixty-nining without me?" James teased.

"Hurry up!" April said. "There's a car coming up on our right!"

"What are you doing with your seatbelt still on?" Mimi asked, glancing over at me.

"We're on the highway!" I yelled. "I can't unbuckle my seatbelt, that's dangerous! And do you know how much a ticket like that costs?"

James was giggling like a maniac. I hoped he still had his eyes shut tight. I pulled the red dress over my head to shimmy it on.

"*Woooooooooooooooooooooo!*"

"Shit!" April said.

"What is it?" I asked, panicking. The tight dress was stuck over my head and I couldn't see anything.

"It's a car full of guys on the right."

"*Show us your tits!*"

I blushed hard underneath the dress. At least I was wearing underwear. I could take some comfort in that.

"*Take it all off!*"

I heard the window rolling down in the back seat as I tugged the dress down over my shoulders. April leaned over her boyfriend to yell out the window.

"FUCK OFF!" she screamed back at the guys.

"I'm going to run them off the fucking road," Mimi said. I barely had time to yell *no* before she yanked the wheel hard.

"*AHHHHHHHHHHHHHHHH!*"

We all screamed as the SUV swung over into their lane. They honked and slowed down, laughing hysterically.

27

I pulled the dress down the rest of the way, adjusting it over my hips. God, it was a tight dress.

"Ugh," Mimi scoffed. *"Thirsty."*

"One of them is mooning us," April said, turned almost completely around in her seat.

"Hey, you don't get to look at other guys' butts," James said, tickling her side. She burst out laughing.

Despite myself, I giggled as the car with the mooning guy swerved off onto an exit ramp. I looked down at the dress. It looked badass.

...*I* looked badass.

"Thanks, April," I said. "I'll try not to get anything on it."

"What about if a pirate captures you and steals you away into the Pacific?" James teased.

"Then I'll send you an envelope with gold doubloons to pay it back," I said, sticking my tongue out at both him and April.

"Here we are!" Mimi shouted. I looked up.

"This is it?" The border loomed up in front of us, a mess of concrete walls and half-finished construction. I'd never been down this far.

"This is it!" Mimi said. The tires chattered over the rumble strips as we slowed down.

I was flabbergasted at how easy it was to get into Mexico. There was nothing in our way at all. Not even a single border patrol. We pulled up to an automatic gate that lifted up, and we drove right across.

"Wow," I said. "That's... that's all it takes? They didn't check our passports, or—"

"Easy as getting into a parking lot," James said from the back. "It's getting back out that's tough."

He thumbed back over at the exit lanes to get into America. On the other side of the highway, I could see American guards with guns lined up at every exit lane. Customs agents in protective plastic cages. Metal gates stretching fifteen feet high stretched over the sidewalk entrance. Barbed wire everywhere. The setting sun shone over the border wall, glinting off of the long line of waiting cars.

"Wow," I said again. "So that's it? We're in Mexico?"

"Hell yeah! Tijuana, baby!" Mimi hooted.

"Uh, where are we going, exactly?"

"I know this club," Mimi said. "It's super nice. All the rich guys I know in TJ go there."

"What's the cover?" I hadn't brought any money at all in my purse.

"For us? Are you kidding? They let girls in free as long as you don't look trashy."

"Too bad for you, Mimi!" April said, kicking the back of Mimi's seat.

"Hey!"

Mimi laughed, and I began to laugh along. I didn't know what it was, but as soon as we'd crossed the border into Mexico, it seemed like a weight had been lifted off of my shoulders.

Over here, I wasn't plain old Jessica anymore. I could be anything I wanted to be. I could act however I wanted to act. On either side of the bumpy street, throngs of people made their way through the crowded sidewalks. There were fruit stands everywhere, and taco trucks on the corners of the streets. And a million other people who didn't know anything about me.

I looked down at the tight red dress curving over my

hips. This wasn't the old me. I was doing something I wasn't supposed to be doing, for once in my life. And it felt... liberating. Like a breath of fresh air. I rolled down the window, unbuckled my seat belt, and leaned out as far as I could.

"*Viva Mexico!*" I shouted, spreading my arms wide in pure joy. "*Wooooooooooooo!*"

Chapter Five

Vale

When Valentina stepped into the private jet, it was all I could do not to gape. The way she strutted up the aisle made me think she was used to guys taking one look at her and popping their eyes out with a cartoonish _AROOGA_ sound.

Long black hair flowed over her shoulders in waves pinned back loosely from her face. Her features were exotic. Maybe Asian, maybe something else. Her eyes were so dark that it looked like her pupils had swallowed the irises whole. She was wearing a fire-engine red dress with a slit all the way up, hinting at a smooth upper thigh.

She sat down across from me and crossed her legs. The plush leather seats in the small private jet faced each other, and I was pretty sure I knew the color of her underwear.

"You're the man they sent." It wasn't a question, but I nodded anyway.

"You're handsome," she said idly, batting her long dark lashes. The jet engines started up and I glanced out of the window.

"Why do I get the feeling that if I say anything like that to you, something bad will happen to me?"

"You're smart, too," Valentina said, smiling. "El Alfa wouldn't like you even talking to me."

"Excuse me," the flight attendant said, bending down over the back of my seat. "Would either of you like a drink?"

"The Napa Cabernet," Valentina said. She'd obviously flown this plane before.

"Whiskey neat," I ordered.

Valentina waited until the flight attendant disappeared into the back of the plane before leaning forward. Her cleavage spilled over the top of her low-cut dress. I had to focus on the space between her eyes to keep my gaze from drifting. Good practice, I told myself.

"What is your name?" she asked.

"Vale. We're supposed to be—"

"Old family friends. Right. They told me. Vale and Valentina," she mused. She seemed utterly unworried about the ruse. I wondered how easy this plan was going to be to pull off.

"So tell me about your friend. El Alfa," I said.

Valentina shrugged.

"He's a man," she said. "He likes to fuck."

"Anything else?"

"He likes to fuck rough."

The flight attendant came back with our drinks and disappeared again. The plane was empty other than us, and it felt weird to be sitting in the middle of a half dozen empty seats. Valentina sipped her wine as the plane taxied down the runway.

"They said you think he's responsible for some women going missing," I probed.

"I don't think. I *know*."

"What does he do that's so bad?"

Valentina's eyes flashed with something like fear.

"He's a bad man," she said. "He hurts women."

I lifted my whiskey glass and took a swallow. The

amber liquid ran smooth and hot down the back of my throat, burning my stomach as it hit.

"You know why you're bringing me there?" I asked.

She nodded slightly and recrossed her legs.

"They told me all about you," she said.

"Is that right?" I took another swallow of whiskey. "Then you know I'm single."

"Yes." She pressed her lips together.

"What else do you know about me, Valentina?"

"Don't patronize me," she said sharply. The wine in her glass sloshed as the jet began to pull away, the engines roaring. Small planes were always so loud.

I frowned.

"What did they tell you about me?"

"They told me what happened to your last girlfriend," she said. She didn't look at my eyes.

My stomach turned hard as lead.

"They told you that?"

"They told me you killed her." Now she looked directly at me. I would have been worried the flight attendant would hear, but the jets were so loud I could barely hear her myself. "They told me to be careful around you."

I met her gaze as steadily as I could.

"That's good advice," I said.

"Is it true?" Her lashes fluttered like a hummingbird's wings.

My fingers were gripped tight around the glass of whiskey.

"It's true," I said. The plane was moving fast now, the runway speeding by outside of the window.

"Why?"

"Why what?"

"Why did you kill her?" Valentina asked.

The plane bumped once, twice, and then lifted off, its wings flashing bright in the Los Angeles sunshine. I felt my stomach lurch for a moment, and then the feeling stopped. I went to take another swallow of whiskey and found the glass empty. I stared blankly at the bottom of the glass.

"Because," I said, "She tried to kill me first."

The quickest way to Rosarito was through San Diego. We touched down and Valentina led the way out the airplane.

A black Jeep was waiting on the tarmac. I hopped into the back seat. Valentina ignored my hand and climbed in herself. She hadn't said much to me after I'd told her about Jen.

"Where are we going?" I asked, once it was clear we were headed the wrong direction. The driver was silent. "The highway to Mexico is back that way."

"There are cameras all along the border," Valentina explained.

"Yeah? So how the hell are we getting across?"

Valentina only smiled as the Jeep pulled through a gated entrance and parked.

"Oh," I said. I looked at the murky water and shivered. There was something about the ocean that always got my nerves up. "Are you serious?"

"Easier than a passport," Valentina said. She strutted

down the pier to the end, where a white motorboat was
waiting. A man in sunglasses stood at the front of the boat.
The helm, or whatever the hell it's called.

"Come on!" Valentina said, waving at me. I sighed.

"A fucking boat," I said. "Of all things, a fucking
boat."

I clambered down onto the deck and sat down on the
side of the boat Valentina was on. I looked around.

"Isn't there a seatbelt on this thing?" I asked.

Valentina laughed. The man in sunglasses revved the
motor, and I fell sideways as the boat lifted half out of the
water with the force of the engine propelling us.

"Shit!" I cried, hanging onto the edge of the seat. We
sped through the water, passing a dozen small sailboats
and a couple of jetskiers. One of them waved, and the man
in sunglasses waved back.

"You're fine," Valentina said. She shook her dark
hair, obviously enjoying the wind streaming across her
face. "Don't worry, I'll throw you a life jacket if you fall
in."

The boat lifted and fell in a gentle rhythm as it
motored over the choppy water. I tried not to show my
worry. Working for the Feds? Fine. Assassinating a guy?
No problem. But Ten hadn't said anything about having to
get on a fucking boat.

"Is that the inside?" I asked, pointing at the door.
"Can I go inside for this trip?"

"You don't want to be inside the cabin," Valentina
said. "You'll be seasick."

"I'm already seasick," I grumbled, holding onto the
wooden railing. I shouldn't have had another whiskey. I
shouldn't have had the first whiskey.

The boat sped out of the harbor. As we reached the open ocean, I saw something in the water.

"What's that?" I said, pointing. It was a dark form emerging from the water. I swear to God it looked like the Loch Ness monster for a moment.

"Submarine," Valentina said, completely unimpressed. We steered to the side as the dark shape rose up from the water, sending waves ripping through the ocean behind it.

Jesus. A submarine. It was huge. Sheets of water ran down the sides, and as we got closer, the waves from its wake made our boat bob up and down even worse. I held my stomach and tried to think of anything except what would happen if another sub came up right underneath us.

"Fuck," I said, staring at the sunlight glinting off the dark waves. The boat swung out to the open sea. I guessed he was taking us in an arc to avoid any Coast Guard boats, but it looked like we were heading out into fucking nowhere. "Fuck. Fuck. Fuck."

I was still swearing by the time we reached Rosarito. I stumbled off of the boat gratefully onto the pier. Even though I knew better, it felt like the ground was moving under my feet.

"Where are we?" I asked.

"Almost there," Valentina said.

I looked around. This sure didn't look like a billionaire's mansion. Shacks with tin roofs and dingy stucco walls lined the beachside, and the people moving along the pier were dressed in rags, carrying buckets and nets. The smell of fish mixed with the smell of rotting seaweed.

We walked down to the edge of the road, where two

men were taking fish out of their nets and another man was cleaning them. I stepped carefully around the fish guts, trying hard not to slip on the slick concrete. There was a dead dolphin washed up on the rocks near the pier, and a mangy dog was gnawing on the end of its flipper.

"This is *not* El Alfa's place," I said, bile rising in my throat.

Valentina, cool as a cucumber, raised a finger.

"Wait," she said. As though on command, a limo appeared from around the corner. None of the fishermen even looked up from their nets.

We stepped into the limo and it pulled away. Behind me in the mirror, I could see the stray dog still pulling at the dolphin's carcass.

"This place is nuts," I said.

"It's not bad," Valentina said. "You wanted a job, didn't you?"

"Sure. Of course."

I leaned back in my seat. I was acting a part now. The part of a desperate man, eager to do any work that he could. Including whatever dirty work El Alfa had in store.

"Want another drink?" Valentina asked, pulling open the bar at the back of the limo. She poured herself another glass of red wine.

"No thanks," I said, still thinking about the dolphin. My stomach was queasy from the long boat ride in the hot sun. I needed a shower. And a haircut.

We drove up the coastal highway. We passed broken down taquerias sitting right next to luxury high-rise condos. Both kinds of buildings were surrounded with high gates and barbed wire.

"I've never been to Mexico," I said.

"It's beautiful," Valentina said. We passed a liquor store where a man was leaning against the wall, pissing into the gutter. "Well, it *can* be beautiful."

"Is El Alfa's place beautiful?"

"You tell me. We're here," she said, pointing. I looked ahead to where the limo was beginning to pull into the driveway through a swinging gate. Two guards stood on either side of the driveway with AK 47s at their sides. My eyes widened.

Through the gate, down the end of a driveway lined with palms and huge prehistoric succulents, was El Alfa's estate. A white stucco mansion, it was built right into the side of the cliffs. It was all arches and terracotta tile roofs. The walls shimmered bright white in the late afternoon sunshine and ivy crept up from the terracotta pots. The huge mirrored windows reflected the waves in the ocean below.

Beautiful, sure. Surrounded by poverty and filth, but beautiful nonetheless.

As we drove up to the house, I saw four more guards walking in a patrol around the perimeter. We stopped in front of a white marble terrace with steps leading up to the front of the house.

I got out of the limo and watched as Valentina was helped out by two of the guards. She smiled at them and said something in Spanish. One of the guards gestured to me. I tried not to look like I didn't know what the hell I was doing.

"Come on," Valentina said. "He says El Alfa has a job for you."

My heart beat fast. I didn't know what I had been expecting. This was why I was here, after all. But now that

it was happening, I felt like I was getting sucked into
something more dangerous than I'd ever faced before.

Chapter Six

Jessica

"Stop fussing with your dress," Mimi said. "It looks fine."

"It's way too short," I said. I tugged my dress down and the top slipped, exposing way too much cleavage. I tugged it back up and the hem slipped up, exposing my butt. "Ah!"

"Don't worry," Mimi said. "Look at April. Her dress is way shorter than yours."

"Yeah, but she has her boyfriend with her." As though he'd heard us, James cupped his hand around April's ass and squeezed. April squeaked and hit him on the shoulder.

"Come on, people," Mimi said, snapping her fingers. "Look classy. This is a classy establishment."

I looked up at the neon sign above the club. _Bailamos._ That's what the place was called. In front of the door, a huge mountain of a man stood blocking the way. His black polo shirt read "Seguridad."

"Follow my lead," Mimi said. She strutted up to the bouncer. Her gold sequin dress fluttered at her thighs.

"Buenas noches," she said, in an obviously American accent.

The bouncer looked over at the rest of us, sizing us up. He frowned at James, but April clung tightly to her boyfriend's arm. Then he looked at me.

Oh, God. I never went clubbing. Never. What if he

decided not to let us in because of me? I smiled nervously. The bouncer's eyes slid down my body to my skirt. I tugged the hem down hard. Too hard.

My boobs popped right out of my bra and over the top of the tube-top dress.

April gasped. Mimi's dazzling smile froze. I squeaked and yanked the dress back up.

"Oh my God, I'm sorry," I said. I crossed my arms across my chest. "I'm sorry. I don't. I can't. I'm sorry!"

The bouncer started laughing, a booming laugh that made me turn even hotter with embarrassment. He unclipped the rope and winked at me as Mimi yanked us through the doorway.

"Wow, Jessica," James said. "Why did you make me close my eyes in the car? If I'd known I was going to get to see the whole show anyway…"

"Shut up!" I hissed. Mimi and April were falling over each other in laughter in the inside hallway.

"Thanks for taking one for the team," April said.

"Yeah, I am never letting you live this down," Mimi chimed in. "The night Jessica flashed the bouncer to get us into the club!"

"What would your mother think?"

"Oh God, shut up," I said. "Just let me get out of Mexico without flashing anyone else and I'll be okay."

"The night's still young," Mimi said, winking at me. "Don't make promises you can't keep."

"How did I let you drag me into this?"

James pushed open the door to the club. Immediately the loud thrum of the music filled the air. Mimi led the way, in all her gold-sequined glory, and the rest of us followed behind.

YOURS

I stopped dead in my tracks when we were inside. From the outside, I'd thought this was just going to be another seedy Tijuana nightclub. But Mimi had been right. This place was *classy*.

All around the room, there were thin ropes of lights strung across the ceiling, dimly illuminating the dance floor. Lasers pulsed from the front of the room in time where the DJ was standing. Waitresses in short black cocktail dresses moved between the tables around the edges of the club.

The men were in business suits, without exception. Some of them had taken off their suit jackets, but you could tell that this wasn't a place for blue-collar workers. And the women...

"Whew," James said with a low whistle. "You don't have to worry about your dress being too short."

He was right. All of the girls on the dance floor were dressed in the skimpiest, skin-tight outfits I'd ever seen. Most of them weren't wearing bras, their nipples completely visible through the sheer fabrics. One girl who was dancing near us was wearing something that looked like it came out of a dominatrix catalog - tiny black leather straps stretching across her hips and leather nipple tassles.

April punched James on the shoulder, and he winced.

"What?" he said defensively. "I was just looking!"

"Don't look," she said.

"I think I can see her vulva," I said, not bothering to keep the horror out of my voice.

"Let's dance," Mimi said. She yanked me out onto the dance floor, closer to the DJ.

I didn't know how to dance, but I didn't have to. Everyone's attention was drawn to Mimi as she threw her

43

arms in the air and gyrated wildly against me. The sound of the drums pounded in the air overhead. I shifted my weight back and forth in time to the beat and looked around nervously.

Three margaritas later, and I wasn't nearly as worried as I had been. April and James were all over each other on the dance floor, and Mimi was busy picking out the hottest guys in the club that she wanted me to hook up with.

"I'm not going to hook up with anyone!" I told her for the tenth time.

"Why not?" she yelled back over the music.

"That's not really my thing!"

Mimi pulled me closer to her, so close that I could smell not just the tequila on her breath, but also the salt and lime that had washed it down.

"If your whole life is making other people happy, nothing is ever going to make you happy!" she said.

I nodded, not sure how she was going to tie her philosophical notions back to hooking up with the hottie from Ensenada.

"You can't get that from other people," she said, jabbing me in the chest with one finger. "*You* have to find your *own* happiness."

"Deep thoughts by Mimi," I said. "Thank you for that."

"You're welcome!" she yelled. "Now go have fun!"

I grinned. Then I felt a tap on my shoulder and a man's accented voice spoke so close he was almost in my ear.

"Hello there," he said.

Chapter Seven

Vale

"Already?" I asked the guard. "I mean, sure. Yeah. Great."

A job right away? What did El Alfa have in mind for me?

They spoke rapidly in Spanish as we climbed the terrace to the front door. Valentina turned to me, a dangerous look in her eyes.

"He wants you to help with training," she said.

"You start tonight," the guard said, in halting English. "You must wear a suit."

I looked down.

"I'm wearing a suit."

The man scowled.

"A better suit," Valentina explained. "He'll set you up. And you need a haircut."

"I had an appointment today," I muttered, but I followed the guard into the house.

Immediately my wonder turned into something more like awe.

The inside of the mansion was expansive, a classic design. But what made my breath catch in my throat was who was there.

Dozens of beautiful women lounged in every part of the entryway that I could see. Two women sat on a marble bench just in front of us, and many more stood in casual poses down along the hallway. All of them were dressed in white gowns so sheer that I could make out the shape of their nipples. Some of them had leather collars around their necks.

The women in front of us stood up—they were definitely not wearing any panties under those dresses. I tried not to stare.

The guard waved the two women back and motioned for me to come. I looked to Valentina.

"I'll see you later," she purred. "Good luck. I hope you impress El Alfa with your… dedication."

Then she was gone, and a cold fear crept into my chest. We had talked the whole plane ride about our cover story, but I was still worried. This wasn't America, and I was all by myself in the mansion of a madman.

As I followed the guard down the hallway, the women turned to face me, standing in poses that showed off their figures. There were all kinds—dark haired Asian beauties, voluptuous redheads, platinum blondes so rail thin that I could see their shoulder blades. The guard seemed hardly to notice them, and I followed suit, as hard as it was. Were they all escorts?

The guard stopped in front of a door with dark iron bars on the front. He opened the door silently and gestured into the room, where two women sat on a large luxurious bed. They both had dark hair, and they were wearing those same gauzy white dresses. One looked a bit older, but the younger one couldn't have been a whisper over eighteen. I wondered if it was a test.

"They will help you get ready," the guard said.

I nodded and stepped through the door. Although it had opened silently, it closed behind me with a loud clang. I tried not to jump.

YOURS

The women didn't say anything to me as I walked in. I didn't know if they spoke English or not. They took my hand and led me to the bathroom. Everything was white marble and adobe. One of them began to loosen my tie. I bit my lip and didn't say anything as she stripped me down to just my underwear. Then the older one motioned for me to sit on a stool. She held up a pair of scissors.

"Oh, right," I mumbled. "The haircut."

I'd been going to the same barber in Los Angeles for years. That, stupidly enough, was all I could think about as this woman *snip snip snipped* all around my head. What kind of cut was she going to give me? I couldn't look in the mirror until after she was done.

Wow. I brushed the loose hairs off of my shoulders and examined my head in the mirror. She'd given me a short haircut. It wasn't buzzed, but shorter than I was used to. I ran my hand along my scalp, ruffling the spikes of hair. My hair always got lighter at the tips, and now it looked dark blond, like the new James Bond. Not bad.

They let me shower on my own, and when I came out of the bathroom there was a dark charcoal suit waiting for me on the bed, definitely nicer than the one I'd arrived in. The sun had set quickly outside, and the women had already left candles lit for me on the table to supplement the dim light of the lamps.

I realized, looking out of the dark window, that I didn't know exactly where I was in the mansion. There had been a hallway with a stairwell that went down, another set of stairs going up past the main entrance, but I didn't know where either of those stairs led.

More than that, I hadn't seen any doors that looked like they led to the outside. And from the outside, there weren't any doors leading in except the entrance. I didn't have a backup exit strategy. That was dangerous. I promised myself to take a better look around later.

I pulled the suit on quickly, smoothing down the fabric as I looked at myself in the side mirror. It was a perfect fit, and the material was as high quality as any I'd ever seen. Fine knit wool and a satin lining.

"Do you like it?"

The booming voice echoed through the room. It was a deep voice, heavily accented.

I turned to see the man I had come here to kill.

El Alfa. He stood in the doorway of the bedroom with his arms crossed, two guards in all black suits standing behind him. He had a thick black mustache and a gut that had probably been created one dinner at a time from too much tequila and lobster.

"It's very nice," I said. Every muscle of mine was on high alert. This was a dangerous man. A man who killed and got away with it. I had to be careful.

"Good," El Alfa said, stepping forward. We shook hands, and he looked me directly in the eyes. I met his gaze, not flinching as his hand squeezed mine.

He was looking for uncertainty, I knew. He was looking for fear. I wasn't going to give him either.

"They said you have a job for me," I said. I wanted to seem a little less experienced than I was, a little more eager. Someone who was willing to do anything.

Was I willing to do anything? I didn't know yet. Ten hadn't told me much, and Valentina had told me even less. Now it was time to find out what kind of man El Alfa really was.

"Yes," El Alfa said. He smiled, a toothy white smile,

and a chill dripped down the back of my spine. "Come with me."

Chapter Eight

Jessica

I spun around, my hair flying back into the air, to see who had tapped me on the shoulder. A tipsy dizziness hit me as my eyes refocused on the face in front of me. He had a thinly clipped beard and dark Mexican eyes that looked me over sensually.

He was young and more than kinda cute, and I looked back over my shoulder to see if Mimi approved. But she had already disappeared with her new dance partner into the crowd. I guessed that meant she had approved, and was going to leave me to _make my own happiness_. Whatever the hell that meant.

"Can I buy you a drink?" the guy asked, his voice only slightly accented.

"Sure!" I said, with a bright smile. He motioned towards the bar and I followed him through the crowd. My heart thumped. What was I doing? Was I actually letting some random guy buy me a drink? Yes, yes, I was, I told myself. This was the new Jessica.

I watched as he ordered for us, careful to make sure he didn't put anything in my drink. Years of reading horror stories about date rape had me on edge. But he came back with two bottles of beer, lime wedges tucked into the necks.

"Thank you!" I said.

"What?"

"Thank you!" I yelled.

I sipped at my beer as we danced. I didn't really like beer, but the margaritas had already taken the edge off, and the lime made it taste almost like Sprite. I thought that after we finished our drinks, we could maybe go outside and talk, get to know each other better. I didn't know how to pick guys up at a club.

Miguel—that was his name, Miguel—didn't seem to want to talk, though. He asked me a few questions about myself, and I answered dutifully, but all he wanted to do was dance. He pulled me into his arms and led me in a weird, salsa-style of dancing. I tried to follow as best as I could, but I was tipsy and he wasn't very good at dancing. Still, it was fun. I was starting to let myself let loose a little bit. When they played a song I knew, I threw my arms up in excitement.

"I love this song!" I cried out. Miguel laughed and danced along with me. I spun around, shaking my ass in time to the music. My dress slipped down, showing a lot more boob than I was normally comfortable with. Oh, well. That was Mimi's fault. Either way, I didn't want a repeat of the bouncer incident. If I tried to fix my dress, I would just end up mooning my new potential pickup.

"You look beautiful!" Miguel yelled, leaning close to my ear. In his accent, it sounded like *Bee-yoo-tee-fool*.

"Thank you!" I yelled back.

His hand was on my waist. How had it gotten there? I didn't know. I swayed to the beat, the air hot on my face. Maybe Mimi was right. Maybe I should try to hook up with someone. Just make out for a bit outside, maybe. Miguel was pretty darn cute. I grinned stupidly at him and leaned even closer.

"You look handsome too!" I said.

Miguel nodded, but then his eye caught something past my shoulder. The smile faded from his face.

"Very handsome!" I said, but he wasn't paying attention to me anymore. His hand fell away from my waist.

"What is it?" I asked, frowning. He shook his head. His eyes were still locked upward. I turned around. Was there another girl he was interested in? But there weren't any girls up on the balcony where he was looking. All I saw was a fat Mexican guy in a suit. Next to him was a taller man with close-cropped dark blond hair, and behind them were a few other men dressed all in black.

"Are those your friends?"

I turned around, but Miguel was already backing away from me. There was fear on his face.

"Goodbye," he said. "I—I have to go."

"Wait, *what?*"

I looked down to see if my boobs had popped out of my dress. Nope, that wasn't it. I turned back. The men up on the balcony were talking to each other, looking down at the dance floor.

The tall one, the one with dark blond hair, made eye contact with me. His eyes were a light blue, so piercing that his stare sent shivers down my back. The fat Mexican man noticed me looking, and turned away. All of the other men walked off into the shadows with him.

"What the hell was that?" I asked, standing suddenly alone in the middle of the dance floor.

Chapter Nine

Vale

We walked into one of El Alfa's clubs, and I felt my chest tighten under the new suit. It was hot upstairs, and the floor under our feet vibrated with the heavy beat of the club music. I didn't know what El Alfa wanted me to do, but I hoped that it didn't involve anything too terrible. He'd been quiet the whole way over here, and it made me nervous with anticipation.

I mean, I'd killed men before, sure, but they'd been assignments. I knew that they were bad people when I killed them. Now, though, I didn't know what El Alfa was planning, or who he was planning to do it to. If I had to torture an innocent person to gain his trust, could I do it? I'd told Ten that I could do anything, but even I had my limits.

I just didn't know exactly what those limits were.

"What are we doing here?" I asked finally.

El Alfa patted me on the shoulder and motioned me through the back rooms of his club. In one room, a man was counting out piles of hundred dollar bills. In the other, two strippers were all over some businessman. He leaned forward and snorted a line of coke off one of the stripper's thighs. Drugs? I could do that, if that's what was needed to show I was trustworthy. But El Alfa led me past those rooms, all the way out to the main club.

"We are going to bring back some girls tonight," he said, cracking his knuckles. "Someone for you to train."

"Train?"

"You saw all of my lovely ladies in the house, yes?" he asked. I nodded. "Well, they are not always so obedient at first."

It was then that everything clicked into place. Ten hadn't been completely honest with me when he'd talked me into this assassination. Or maybe he was being honest with me, and he only suspected the dangerous truth.

El Alfa wasn't just dealing drugs. He was dealing in something much more dangerous… sex slavery.

I'd heard about this kind of operation before. Some of the drug cartels were moving into the sex trade. They kidnapped women and beat them into submission. Or, as El Alfa put it, they *trained* them. Then they would sell the girls abroad to the highest bidder.

As I moved farther into the club with El Alfa, I thought over what I knew about sex slavery. Asia was a hot market. Lots of businessmen there with too much money and nowhere to spend it. It was risky to kidnap white girls and sell them, but the cartels who managed to do it commanded a high profit margin.

Sex slavery. The thought of *training* a kidnapped girl made me sick to my stomach.

"I understand," I said, trying not to let my disgust show on my face. I set my mouth in a serious expression. I could control my face perfectly. I didn't let a single muscle tic, not even when El Alfa licked his lips and looked out over the crowd.

"This is the fun part," he said, breathing heavily. "You get to pick. What is your fancy?"

What a fucking bastard. I couldn't wait to shoot him in the goddamn face. But I had to get him alone, somewhere where I had a clear escape path, or wait for the raid. So far, his guards had been breathing down my neck, even though I wasn't armed at all.

We stood on the balcony overlooking the dance floor. There were dozens of hot women writhing to the beat. My eye caught one of them, a cute curvy brunette in a tight red dress. She turned to look at me, and her dark brown eyes took my breath away.

Christ. She couldn't have been more than college age. I turned away quickly, but El Alfa had already seen me looking at her.

"That one?"

I shrugged. My mouth was like paste. I couldn't torture a young woman like that. Jesus.

"Maybe another one," I said, but I said it too late.

"No, you are right," El Alfa said. He leaned forward on the balcony, his finger scratching his thick mustache. "Good to train."

"Really? Why?" I couldn't look down, couldn't meet her eyes again. I'd sentenced her to hell, and I didn't even know her.

"She looks innocent, but she's wearing a whore's dress."

I swallowed hard and looked again. She was talking to another girl on the dance floor. One hand tugged down on her dress. The innocence of the futile gesture made my heart clench. *I'm sorry.*

"Yes," El Alfa said, nodding. "I think it'll be an easy one to train."

He clapped his hands, and one of his guards pulled out a pill bottle. He tossed it to me and I caught it.

"What's this?"

57

"Drugs. Makes them willing. Bring her out back when you can, and we'll leave from there."

I held the pill bottle tightly in my hand. Probably a date rape drug. I was aghast at how nonchalant El Alfa seemed to be about drugging girls without even knowing what dose to give. I supposed that he didn't care if he killed a few of them, anyway. My pulse jumped up a notch and my fingers itched at my side where my gun was normally holstered. It was hard to keep my face straight.

"Are you good, Americano?" El Alfa asked. His greasy mustache creased upward into a sick smile. "You have this under control?"

"Of course."

Control. I breathed in, then out, remembering my training. I had to brace myself for what might be coming. Ten said that I would have to do El Alfa's dirty work, and this was as dirty as I could have imagined. But if that was what it took to get rid of this asshole, I could handle it.

I could handle anything.

Chapter Ten

Jessica

"Hey!"

Mimi's voice brought me back down to the dance floor. Her cheeks were flushed from dancing and alcohol, and her long dark hair swished over her shoulders messily. I realized that I probably looked just as ridiculous.

"Where's your new boyfriend?" Mimi asked.

I shrugged.

"I don't know. He said he had to go."

"Bummer."

"Where's April?"

"Out back, puking up her third margarita. I swear, that girl is such a lightweight."

"She's not alone out there, is she?" I asked quickly.

"Nah, James is with her."

"Good." I breathed out. I wasn't a lightweight myself, but the bar here poured their drinks *strong*. The room was spinning whenever I turned around too quickly. I looked up again to see if the blond guy was still there up on the balcony, but there was nobody there.

"Hello? Hello? Earth to Jessica?"

"Sorry, what?"

"Did you want to come out and smoke with us?"

I frowned.

"You don't smoke, Mimi."

Mimi rolled her eyes and pinched two fingers to her lips, puffing her lips out.

"Not cigarettes, dummy."

My jaw dropped.

"You don't mean… *pot?*" I whispered the last word.

Mimi burst into drunken laughter.

"Claro que si!" she said, dancing around in circles and shaking her gold sequined hips. "La marijuana… la *ganja…*"

"Shh! Isn't that illegal here?"

"Nah. It's like, the national plant."

"But—"

"I'll see you later, okay? Or I'll meet you back at the hotel tomorrow, just go with April and James."

Before I could protest again, Mimi had skipped off toward the front entrance. She caught a guy around the waist and he laughed, pulling her close for a kiss. She squealed and slapped his ass. They left the club, falling all over each other.

Shit. I looked out to the front entrance, then back across the dance floor. April was outside, she'd said? I should go make sure she was okay. James was a good boyfriend sometime, but he didn't have nearly the experience I did at holding back hair when a friend was puking up her guts.

As I looked around, it seemed like Miguel was nowhere to be found. My best chance at a hookup was gone, and I didn't really care. I wasn't about to lose my virginity to some random guy in Mexico, anyway. I felt bad about not thanking him again for the drink, and my mom's voice rang in my head—*Always be polite! Be grateful!*

Well, I was grateful she wasn't here to see me now.

I wandered back through the dance floor, pushing my way past writhing bodies to get to the back hallway. There, couples were pressed against the wall doing all kinds of things that I'd only read about in books. The bathroom door for the girls' room was open, and I poked my head inside to see if April was there.

Two women looked up from the bathroom sink. Their eyes were glazed over, and I saw a smudge of white powder under the nose of the nearest one. She lifted an arm and spoke rapidly in Spanish.

"Sorry!" I said. I turned around and ran straight into a wall.

No, it wasn't a wall. It was a man's chest. A dark suit, so expensive that I cringed at the smudge of lip gloss that had come off on his lapel. As I lifted my head and opened my mouth for yet another apology, I froze.

It was the guy from upstairs. His eyes were icy blue, and his dark blond hair was slicked back. Every feature of his was drawn tight, but despite his cold expression, something in his face made my body respond instantly with warmth. I swallowed hard, my heart beating double time. There were words on my tongue, I just couldn't find them. The way he was looking at me made my body clench with desire.

"Ex—excuse me," I said. I licked my lips. "I was looking for my friend—"

"You're beautiful," he said. "Dance with me."

It was an order, not a question. The words went through my body with a shiver. He put an arm around my waist and drew me close to him as we moved back onto the dance floor.

The pressure of his hand against the small of my back sent thrills through my core. We swayed to the music, our hips in synchrony. I felt dizzy with desire as the beat thudded through my chest. His palm was hot, even through the fabric of my dress. Was that the reason I felt so overheated?

I looked up into ice blue eyes that bored into me like a drill. This guy—this guy wasn't dancing with me, was he? His white shirt stretched out over a chiseled body that could have been a football quarterback's. His arms were all muscle, and his features were dramatic and dark—dark eyebrows slanting over his light blue eyes, dark stubble on his jaw. He was beauty incarnate. As we moved to the music, I let him draw me closer.

Our bodies pulsed against each other, and as the song ramped up to a thick, heavy beat, he ran his hand down my back. Every nerve inside of me was shot through with electricity. As the first song ended and the next began, he stepped back closer to the back hallway, pulling me along.

"Um, thanks for dancing with me," I said. Sheesh. Way to go, Jessica. Just what your mom would think to say. But he only smiled back at me.

"The pleasure's all mine," he said.

I felt like pumping my fists in the air and cheering for myself. Why had I been so unsure about coming to Mexico? This was… this was perfect.

"What's your name?" I asked, tilting my head flirtatiously. I tried to channel my inner Mimi. She would know exactly how to flirt with this kind of guy.

He bent his head down as though he hadn't heard me, although the music wasn't nearly as loud in the back hallway.

"What's yours?"

"Jessica."

"A beautiful name for a beautiful girl." He spun me

around to the music and I turned, laughing. The lights above sparkled and the music filled my ears. This handsome man, this Greek god, was dancing with me— me! I couldn't stop the swelling in my heart.

At the end of the spin, my heel caught a bit on the floorboards and I stumbled. He caught me in his arms, pulling me into a tight embrace against his body.

I gasped. He was hard—I could feel him bulging outward through his pants. His erection pressed into my inner thigh as he held me and brushed my hair off of my shoulder. I thought that he would be embarrassed, but there was no hint of shame in his face, only desire, a fierce, fierce desire. When he bent down and kissed my bare neck, I melted into his arms.

"Jessica," he murmured. Then his hands were in my hair and he was kissing me, kissing me like I'd never been kissed before.

I was a virgin, sure, but I'd had my share of boyfriends. None of them, though, were any match for this. His kiss tore the air from my lungs, and his hands moved down over my body, cupping me, caressing me.

I opened my mouth to let my lips part, and he seized my lips his in his, pressing kiss after kiss. My breath was gone by now, completely gone, but I didn't care. I wanted this kiss to last forever. My hands came up and met with broad shoulders. As he kissed me, some part of me inside ripped free. Maybe it was the margaritas, maybe it was just that I was finally really attracted to a guy for the first time. But I found myself pulling him closer. My fingers tangled in his shirt and I pushed back against him, my lips hot and needy.

He looked like an ice god, and his arms circled me

completely. I lost myself in the heat of the kiss, letting him do whatever he wanted, letting him touch me. Whatever he did, I found myself aching for more.

Finally. That was the word that went through my mind. Finally, I had found a man who set my body on fire with his touch. Finally, I had found a man who was strong and not weak, who could possess me wholly. Finally, all of my dark fantasies were coming true.

I was the luckiest girl in the world.

Chapter Eleven

Vale

Her kiss was so… *urgent*. I'd wanted to draw her in slowly, but I knew from the moment I touched her that it was impossible to wait.

It was strange. She seemed utterly innocent. It was her innocence that had drawn her to me initially—the way she looked around nervously, biting her lip. Even as she danced in the middle of the floor, even as she flirted with another man, I could sense that all of this was something that she wasn't quite ready for. She was a young woman as I imagined a young woman should be. Curious. Testing out her sexuality. But unsure.

I knew that El Alfa could sense it as well as I could. He knew that she would be an easy target. Easy to manipulate, easy to possess. She was a woman who would trust me up until the very last moment, too far, until it was too late to escape. Trusting, innocent. The perfect victim.

But there was something else to her. When she looked up into my face, I saw something change inside her expression. A flash of dark ferocity across her eyes. Maybe… maybe she wasn't so innocent after all.

There was only one way to find out.

As she moved in my arms, my cock throbbed. I wanted to pin her back against the wall and take her right then and there. Instead, I turned my hip and pressed myself into her. It was a bold move, and I wanted to see how she would react to me.

She swallowed hard as I pressed my cock against her thigh. Startled, she moved back as though she was going to pull away... then stopped. Her lips parted, but she didn't move away from me. She stayed there, her gorgeous curves teasing my cock with the slow friction of her hips swaying to the beat.

Goddamn. I was going to come right then and there if she kept moving like that. She had to know what she was doing to me. Poor girl. Poor, sweet, perfect girl.

"Jessica," I murmured. Her chestnut hair swept across my hand and her hip tortured my aching cock with slow circles.

Wait, I wanted to say, as I dove into the sweetest kiss. Her lips were hot and full and wanting, and I tore all the sweetness from them that I could. A soft needy noise escaped her lips, making me throb hard against her. Fuck, she was beautiful. So, so beautiful.

Wait, I wanted to say, as I drew her even closer. My hands cradled her, moving down over her warm skin. The end was coming for her, all too soon. I could see the men waiting outside in the alley in my mind's eye. They were waiting for me to bring her out, like a lamb to slaughter.

Then something in her shifted, *changed.* She'd been so complacent before, so gentle. In the middle of our kiss, though, she began to press forward. Her hands pulled at the fabric of my shirt, and her eyes lit up with a fiery passion. Her breasts pressed against my chest and I could feel her nipples, hard through the fabric. God, I'd never wanted a woman so much before.

Wait, I wanted to say. Wait, because the path I'm leading you down ends in a dungeon. Wait, because you only have a few minutes left as a free woman, and every kiss draws us closer to the exit.

Wait, because I don't want this to be over yet.

When I pulled back from the kiss, her eyes were blurred with passionate need. My groin throbbed as she eased herself away from my body. For a single second, when she was looking up into my eyes, I thought she could see right down through my carefully crafted facade. She knew, she *had* to know. She would run away from me now, and I would let her go.

But she didn't leave, and I couldn't postpone the inevitable any longer. I swallowed the lump in my throat, knowing that I had to lead her to the trap waiting for us outside.

"Let's go outside and get some fresh air," I said.

Forgive me.

Chapter Twelve

Jessica

I was oblivious to anything but the fire between us until he pulled back out of the kiss. I felt him tense under me as we leaned against the wall.

"Outside?" I repeated breathlessly.

"Sure. You were looking for your friend?" he asked, a hint of a smile on his face.

Oh, God. April must be puking really bad.

"Yeah," I said, blinking away my dizziness. "I, uh—"

"The back entrance is down this way. We could use a breather anyway, huh?"

He turned and pointed down the hall, past the bathrooms. I shuffled past him with a mumble of thanks, adjusting my dress. I was too tipsy to be wearing heels.

There was another man in a suit standing in front of the back door. As I came closer, I saw him lift his eyes to look at something over my shoulder. Then he nodded and stepped aside, opening the door.

I stepped forward to what looked like an alleyway, but then something made me pause. Some instinct. What was the man in the suit looking at? I turned my head quickly. Dizziness swept through me as I looked up into icy blue eyes.

"You—"

He shoved me back through the doorway so hard that I didn't have any time to cry out. I tumbled out into the alley, catching myself on the rough asphalt with my hands. My palms scraped and a burning pain shot through my arm. I heard the alleyway door slam behind us.

What the hell!?

The blond man yanked me to my feet, pulling me up by the arm as though I weighed nothing. I opened my mouth to scream, but I only got out a yelp before his hand was over my mouth. I struggled, kicking hard, but he held me tight against his chest. One of the other guards came forward and clasped a collar around my neck. A collar?! I kicked out again and got the guard in the shin. But the black leather collar was still tight around my neck.

"You didn't drug her."

The voice came from behind us, and when the blond man turned with me in his arms, I saw who had spoken. The fat guy from upstairs, the one with the mustache.

"I didn't have time. She was heading out here anyway."

Then my eyes refocused, and I saw April and James. They were both on their knees, gags tied around their mouths, with two of the men in black standing behind them. The men—*Oh God*. The men had guns tucked into their belts. I hadn't noticed before.

Behind them, there were two black SUVs parked up against the curb, blocking the alleyway.

April was sobbing silently. Her mascara ran down onto the cloth gag and there was a collar around her throat just like mine. James looked up at me with fear in his eyes. There was a huge bruise on the side of his face. My throat constricted.

Jesus. They're going to kidnap us. All of the stories I'd heard about Americans getting kidnapped and held for ransom came flooding back into my mind. Stories about fingers getting chopped off and sent back as a warning. All of a sudden, I was completely sober.

The fat man stepped in front of me. I wriggled backwards, but the blond man holding me was way too strong for me to even think about getting loose. Then the fat man reached a hand out and stroked my chin. I gulped as his fingers ran down my throat, down past my collarbone.

When he yanked the top of my dress down, I moaned into the hand that was gagging me and pushed away, but there was nowhere to go. He squeezed my tit so hard it hurt.

"Good choice," he said, nodding with a smile that made my bones turn to ice. "Gag her."

That was it. I wasn't going to get taken that easily. I bit down hard on the blond man's hand. My teeth sunk into his palm and he shouted, pulling his hand away. His grip loosened just enough for me to send one good kick to his knee. He dropped me. I jumped sideways, a scream halfway out of my throat, before he caught me again. This time one of the other men stuffed a handful of fabric into my mouth and tied a gag around the back of my head. I kicked, but the blond man only held me tighter.

"What about those two?" the blond man asked, as he held me back from running. He was talking about April and James. April was still sobbing.

"Take the girl."

The other men in black suits pulled April to her feet. She started screaming from behind her gag, hoarse muffled screams. How long had they been out here? I met her eyes for only a second. Then the men opened up the back of one of the black SUVs and shoved her inside, slamming the door behind her.

James struggled, but his hands were tied behind his back and there were two men on either side of him holding him down by the shoulders. He couldn't do anything. My heart pounded faster.

"And this one?"

The fat man with the mustache glanced down. James went white as the man stood over him with no trace of mercy.

"Kill him."

Chapter Thirteen

Vale

"Kill him."

One of El Alfa's henchmen stepped forward, his hand already on his gun. Jessica wrenched back in my arms, trying desperately to twist out of my grasp. It wouldn't do any good. I wasn't about to let her go. But she didn't have to see this. I pushed her toward the SUV that we'd come in. She screamed from behind the gag, her eyes wide as she craned her head to see the boy. I shut the door behind her quickly, but she pressed her face up against the window, still trying to make herself heard from behind the gag.

I turned, standing in front of her view. The henchman had taken the gun from his holster and was stepping toward the boy.

What shitty luck. He should have let his girlfriend go outside alone to puke. If he hadn't been with her, he wouldn't be dead. My mind kept cycling excuses, trying to keep calm. In control.

I clasped my hands loosely in front of me. Any pity I felt for him was locked down so deeply that I couldn't even feel it, not really. My face was smooth, I knew, smooth and controlled. If El Alfa wanted to see how I reacted to a murder, he would be sorely disappointed.

But, as it turned out, he wanted to see more from me.

"Wait."

All of the men looked up at El Alfa's words. He

reached out and took the gun from his henchman's hand.

"But—"

"Hush," El Alfa said to the man. The man looked up at him with a scowl on his face, like he was a child that had just been reprimanded, but that expression quickly disappeared. El Alfa hefted the gun in his hand.

Then he held it out to me.

My eyes flicked from the gun to his face. He didn't mean—

"You are new here," El Alfa said, his voice rasping over my nerves. "Take it."

My jaw started to clench, but I forced myself to relax. I held out my hand and El Alfa set the gun down on my open palm. I wrapped my hand around the gun, my finger stroking the side of the trigger. As I hefted it, El Alfa gripped my wrist. His palm was hot and sweaty but the grip was an iron vise.

"You have killed before?" he asked me.

I forced myself to look at him levelly, even as my heart sank. He wouldn't make me do this. He couldn't. And yet as I stood there, the metal of the gun warming in my hand, I knew that he was capable of this, this and so much more. His tongue darted out, small and pink beneath his oily black mustache.

"Yes," I said.

"Good," he said. He let go of my hand. The place where he had gripped me went cool. "Then this is a good chance for you to show me what you know."

What I knew? My mind reeled forward all of my training. How to kill someone with a rope, a knife, a gun. I knew all of the body parts that hurt most to be shot. If you want information, you break someone's finger or shoot them in the knee. Avoid the femoral artery, or they'll die too quickly. If you want someone to die slow, you shoot them in the stomach. If you want them to die fast—

"*Mmmmm!*"

The kid on the ground was past scared. The front of his pants had gone dark with urine, and his chest was shuddering with silent sobs behind his gag. He was young. Jesus, so young. Twenty, twenty-two at most.

The men I was sent to assassinate were always like El Alfa. Old, fat, and evil as fuck. But this one—he was just a boy. I had to control myself, or my emotions would bubble up to the surface. The thought reverberated in my head.

Control yourself.

I examined the gun, stretching out the seconds he gave me before I had to do anything. A Glock, the black metal dull in the dim light.

My eyes flicked up to El Alfa. Could I shoot him right now? I hadn't thought an opportunity would come up so quickly. Yet here I was, holding a gun, with my target standing right in front of me.

No. I couldn't. There were four men standing next to us, apart from El Alfa himself. I could probably take out two of them, but they had been trained well—they were standing apart from each other so that there was no way to get them at the same time. Two more men driving the SUVs, three more in the backs of the cars. And that's not even counting club security. This was El Alfa's club, after all. A volley of gunfire would bring them running. And the cars were blocking the only exit from the alley—

"Well?"

I looked up at El Alfa. I'd already stalled too long. It

was impossible now. His beady eyes bored into mine, daring me to refuse him. Goddammit. I had a gun in my hand, for Chrissakes. I could shoot him in the face and then what? I'd be killed, and the two girls would get whisked off to God knows where, and the raid would be shot. No. I had to do this.

"Thanks for trusting me," I said with a smirk that hurt my face. I cocked the gun as I stepped behind the sobbing boy. I couldn't save him. Couldn't save him.

I lifted the gun up to aim it at the poor kid's head. From the SUV, I heard a muffled pounding, but I didn't lift my head to look at it. If I saw either of the girls, I wouldn't be able to do it. For all of my rational thoughts, I couldn't help but feel a shudder run through my spine.

Fuck you, Ten, I thought. Fuck you for sitting in your office and giving orders that you would never have to carry out yourself. Fuck you for all of this.

Control. Take control.

The barrel of the gun pressed against the base of his skull. I would make it quick.

He's just a boy.

I shoved down the feeling that threatened to sting the backs of my eyes. I shut it down and locked it away. There was only the gun and the kid, and the darkness swirling up inside me.

It always came when I killed, this dark feeling. It took me over, like a deep instinct I never had to be taught. Lots of people know how to kill, but when the time comes, they freeze. I'd spent my whole life training myself not to freeze. Now, as the darkness swept through my body, my arm, my fingers, I let it come and drive away the empty terror I felt at killing an innocent.

My body relaxed. I didn't shake. This bullet needed to be perfect if I wanted to kill him painlessly.

Control yourself.

I did it. God forgive me, I did it, and the world darkened as my finger pulled the trigger. The boy fell, and the back of his head was gone, and his blood was flowing out black onto the street, black like oil. My stomach turned, but I kept control.

Then it was all over, and El Alfa was taking the gun back, and his men were pulling the body away.

I got into the car, waiting for the darkness to loosen its grip around my chest. The echoes of the gunshot rang in my ears as we drove off, and in the back of the SUV Jessica was screaming from behind her gag.

I took a deep breath, but it felt like I wasn't getting any oxygen. The dark tide that had swept up into me wasn't ebbing away like it normally did after a kill. And then I realized what she was screaming behind her gag, her voice muffled.

"Monster!" she was screaming, her throat hoarse with sobs.

Monster. Yes, that's what I am.

I stared hard out of the window at the neon signs passing by and tried not to think about what I had done.

It wasn't my first kill, true.

But it sure as hell felt like it.

Chapter Fourteen

Jessica

The man with the blue, blue eyes lifted the gun and put it against the back of James' head. My mouth went dry. I had been kicking against the door of the SUV, but now I stopped. No. He wasn't going to shoot him. This was all a bad dream. A nightmare. I was going to wake up any second, and then—

Then the gun bucked, and the sound came through the car window. It hit me like a wave, and James fell over, *flopped* over, his head turning to the side as he fell, bloody. I could hear myself screaming through my gag as it happened, and I couldn't stop.

Then the man who shot him stepped in front of my view. He was looking into the window, right at me, but he didn't see me. I don't think he saw anything.

His eyes looked totally blank. Like a dead man's eyes. *A monster.*

And I'd… I'd kissed him.

I'd kissed this man, this killer, this monster. I wanted to throw up. Behind my gag, I could feel the bile rise in my throat. If I threw up now, I'd probably choke and die. Instead, I closed my eyes and pressed my forehead against the glass of the window. I couldn't stop screaming at the man as he came into the car, and my screams came out like gargled sounds but I couldn't stop myself. He had killed James.

James. Oh, God. James.

"Let's go," the fat man said. The engine roared and I fell back against the side of the door.

I didn't know where they were taking us, but I knew that wherever it was, I didn't want to go there.

Chapter Fifteen

Vale

The moon was shining when we reached El Alfa's estate. In the blue light of the night, the marble gleamed like ice and the palm trees waved dark shadows, their spiked leaves like fingers reaching out to grab us.

I was still thinking about the kid that I'd killed. I'd never killed an innocent before. Never.

My mouth tasted like chalk as I got out of the car. My hands ached from clenching the steering wheel so hard. I wanted to punch something, to get that dark cloud out of my system, but I couldn't. Not here.

El Alfa snapped his fingers and the men dragged the two girls from out of the backs of the cars. They went in front of us. The one I'd danced with, Jessica—she was the one who struggled the most. She was kicking the whole way, but her friend let herself be pulled along without any protest, like a dog that had been beaten too many times to care about fighting back.

We went up the marble steps behind them, and the huge doors in front opened, spilling out a flood of yellow light from inside.

The girls in white gauze dresses scattered in front of us as we walked. None of them looked up at the girls who were bound and gagged. I wondered how many of them had arrived this way themselves. I wondered how many of them had watched their boyfriends get killed in front of their eyes.

We reached the end of the hallway. There was an opening there, with stairs leading down into the blackness. A dim yellow light flickered at the top of the stairs, lighting only the few top steps. The man holding Jessica stopped at the top, and she looked back at me. There was such pleading in her eyes that it made my body grow hot. I couldn't break my cover.

I turned my eyes away to the yellow light. An electric bulb that flickered, a fake torch. I stared at it until the light burned the sickness out of my stomach and I could look down. The man was dragging Jessica down the stairs, then her friend. El Alfa motioned for me to go down the steps. I paused at the top stair, but only for a moment. I could feel his eyes burning into me as we descended down into that maw, swallowed alive by the stony darkness.

We went down the staircase slowly and carefully. It was barely lit with yellow electric torches on the walls, and I found myself putting my hand out to keep my balance as I made my way down the steep stone stairs. Upstairs everything was marble, but down here was only gray, gray rock.

At the bottom of the stairs, two guards stood with AK 47 machine guns cradled in their arms. The stone floor stretched out farther into a narrow hallway. It could have been a scene from a medieval castle, except for the doors. On alternating sides, shiny metal doors staggered like teeth all the way down the hallway. The only sound was the high scream coming from behind Jessica's gag.

El Alfa came up next to me. I suppressed a shudder as he chuckled.

"You did very well tonight," he said. I realized dully that he was talking to me.

"Thanks," I said.

"I want you to see what we do here. The girls upstairs, they are all very obedient, yes?"

"Yes." I wasn't about to contradict him. They didn't seem obedient, I thought. They seemed scared.

"Yes. That's all my doing. I have a very good training program for them. My whores are the best submissives. You see?"

"Yes."

The first henchman was already hauling Jessica's quiet brunette friend into one of the cells. He handled her roughly, banging one of her legs into the metal door as they went in. I had to bite my tongue, but El Alfa didn't.

"David!" he yelled. The henchman turned and glared. "Be careful with the merchandise."

The man nodded, his dark eyes flashing anger. I wondered who this man was, who could get away without answering his boss. All of the other goons working for El Alfa seemed to be terrified of him. But this David... he didn't seem to care.

"After you," El Alfa said, again magnanimously gesturing me before him.

We went into the cell. The room was dark, except for a single shaft of light coming down through the window. The window was only a small square cut into the stone, too small to crawl through, too small for a possible escape. But the sun shone through, one small solitary ray of light piercing the darkness.

David was already chaining up the brunette. Jessica's friend. He slapped black leather cuffs around her wrists, the metal clasps locking them into place. The cuffs were attached to chains, and when David pulled at the chains, her hands stretched outward on each side to the walls. Her head hung forward against her chest. They had taken off her gag, but she wasn't screaming. Instead, she was crying softly.

"You may go now, David," El Alfa said, almost gently. David looked up at me, and I thought I saw a glance of something in his eye. Jealousy, maybe. But then El Alfa was moving toward the girl, and I paid attention to him instead.

"The first thing we teach them is how to kneel," El Alfa said. "They must acknowledge you as a master."

He gripped the girl's chin and jerked it upward. Her eyes were clenched shut, the mascara still running down her cheeks. When El Alfa loosened her chains, her arms hung limply at her sides.

"Look at me, stupid girl," he said. She only sobbed harder.

He slapped her across the face. I suppressed the urge to reach out and give him a taste of violence. Control. I had to keep control.

"Look at me."

Now she looked up dully, the tears streaming across her cheeks.

"Kneel."

She shook her head no, and El Alfa punched her in the stomach, then caught her before she could fall. Yanking her up with one hand, he took hold of her dress with the other and tore. She screamed as her dress turned into shreds. Her underwear was pink, I saw. Pink with small white daisies. I felt sick.

"No!" she cried. "I'll do it! I'll do it!"

She fell to the ground, kneeling awkwardly. El Alfa

kicked her in the side. She curled over.

"Sloppy girl. Next time, obey me right away or I'll take more than your clothes."

She whimpered.

"I'll make her obey," David said, stepping forward boldly. El Alfa shook his head.

"Don't feed her. We'll work on her tomorrow."

David rubbed at the side of his neck as he stood back dejectedly. He had a sunburn, and where his fingers scratched, white curls of skin flecked off of his neck. When he saw me looking at him, he dropped his hand and looked away.

"Come," El Alfa said. He was talking to me. "I will show you a girl who already knows how to obey her master."

He opened the door across the hall. Inside, an Asian girl was curled up on the floor. I could see that she wasn't chained at the wrists but at the throat. A thick black collar wrapped around her neck, attached again to two chains hanging off the walls.

El Alfa snapped his fingers. Immediately the girl scrambled up, her eyes bleary with sleep. There was a dark bruise on her stomach.

"You know how to kneel, don't you?" he said.

"Yes, master." Fear flashed in her eyes.

"Kneel for me."

She bent down slowly, her back rigidly straight. When her knees touched the ground, her body folded forward. Her forehead bent down, almost touching the ground. Her hands stretched out in front of her, palms upward as though begging for something. If I had seen her anywhere else, I would have thought it was a yoga pose.

She held the position, her hands trembling only slightly, as El Alfa walked around her. He nudged at one foot that was angled slightly outward and she immediately straightened out.

"There. That's how they should do it. Not perfect, of course. You can ask any of the girls upstairs if you want a proper demonstration."

"They all have the—uh, the training?"

I had to act interested. I had to act like I wanted this job. Jesus, it was hard. I realized why two of Ten's men had already died in this place. If I didn't keep myself completely in line, I would be next.

"That's right. Once they're ready, we let them upstairs."

I nodded, trying not to look as sick as I felt.

"You did well tonight," El Alfa continued, "but there are many things harder to do than to kill a man. To get a woman to obey you, for instance."

He chuckled at his own joke and I put on an acid smile, feigning amusement.

"So," he said. "We will see if you picked out the right girl tonight."

"What do you mean?"

He led me back out into the hallway and opened yet another door.

My heart fell as I saw Jessica already in chains. She was pulling hard at her cuffs, and her gag was still in.

"I think you may be in for some trouble," El Alfa said. He tore off the gag and Jessica began to scream.

"Help!"

He slapped her, then shoved the gag back into her mouth.

"Take the gag off before you leave her tonight," he said, winking conspiratorially at me. "That way she'll scream herself hoarse. It'll be easier to work with her then."

"What do you mean, work with her?"

"You have control over this one," he said. His grin was sickening. "Good luck getting her to kneel. I think it will take more than a few hours for this one. You'll want to get her out of her clothes. Most girls listen better when they're naked."

"Wait," I said, my mind spinning from all of the orders. "You mean, she's—"

"Yours."

"Mine?"

Jessica met my gaze from behind her gag. Hatred burned in her eyes.

"Yours to control. Yours to train. This is a test, eh? To see if you are good at this job. You are good with a gun, but I have many guns already. I need trainers."

The air in the room was cool down here, but I was still struggling to breathe.

This was it? This was the job I was sent here to do? I'd expected drug trafficking. I'd expected violence. But I hadn't expected... this.

"Keep her pretty," El Alfa was saying. "No guns down here, no knives, yes? Only hands. My clients pay for top quality. They do not want a broken product. Make her listen to you in whatever way you need to, but keep that in mind."

"Sure," I said. Another set of vague orders from a boss who wasn't telling me the whole truth. I looked down at Jessica. Even with a dirty gag stuffed in her mouth, her

87

hands tied up, her eyes rimmed with tears, she looked beautiful.

I was disgusted with myself for the stirring attraction inside of me when I looked at her. I wanted to scream to her that I wasn't like this, that this wasn't *me*. I was just here to do a job. I was just following orders.

Orders. Right. I had a mission to finish. I turned to El Alfa, who was standing in the doorway. Behind him, David looked at me suspiciously.

"The doors are only for containment. They don't lock," he said, "so make sure you keep her in chains. There are guards always in the hallway, of course, if you need any assistance."

"Thanks," I said, storing the information away in my mind. No locks—it made sense, if they had to empty the place out quickly for raids.

"Have fun," El Alfa said. He seemed hesitant to leave me.

"Oh, I will." I forced myself to plaster on a smile, and it seemed to do the trick. El Alfa smiled back and closed the metal door behind him.

Jessica looked up at me in horror as I turned to her, the smile dropping off of my face.

Chapter Sixteen

Jessica

I'd heard April sobbing next door, and I'd heard them hitting her.

I was trying hard not to go crazy with fright. I couldn't _do_ anything. Yanking at the chains was useless—I'd almost dislocated my wrist the first time I'd tried to wrench free, and a deep bruise was creeping up my forearm.

And now the man from the club was alone with me. He stood in front of me, but I didn't cringe back. I wasn't going to let him bully me.

"My name's Vale," the man with the blue eyes said. "I'm going to take off your gag. You heard the guy. Screaming won't do anything. You understand?"

I nodded.

Vale. The Ice God. The man who'd kissed me. The man who killed James. I hated him so much.

He took the gag out of my mouth. I scrounged up as much saliva as I could with my tongue, and spit in his face.

His reaction was quick—he turned his cheek but didn't flinch. Instead, he calmly wiped the spittle away with the back of his hand. I expected that he would hit me. Or slap me. Or even a flash of anger. But there was nothing in his eyes, only a blankness.

"Jessica—"

"How's your hand?" I asked. His palm still bore my bite marks.

Instead of answering, though, he looked down at his hand and rubbed the red mark absently. I thought I saw the glimmer of a smile begin to curve his lips, but then it disappeared.

"I'll never kneel for you," I hissed.

"You will," he said, matter of factly. He paused, as though thinking of something else. "You'll have to."

"*Fuck you. FUCK YOU!*" I screamed.

I screamed it over and over, right into his face, and he stood there, taking it. I'd never hated anyone the way I hated him. I wanted him to hit me. I wanted him to do something—anything. But he just stood there.

Finally, I stopped. My throat was burning, and I felt like I had no more tears left. My whole body had burned through with hatred, and there was nothing left of me but a black shell.

He looked around the cell, and for the first time I realized my surroundings. For some reason, it made me think of a book from one of my intro literature courses. Dante's *Inferno*. The main character had described his descent down through the nine circles of hell. He'd passed through each circle, and the deeper he went, the worse it got.

That was me now. I was in hell. I had let my friends drag me into it, and now I had to pay for it. If only I had listened to my mom…

My mom. I hadn't even talked to her the last time she'd called me. She would find out that I'd lied to her. My heart sank even further. Here I was, and I was paying for my sins, all of them.

"No," I croaked.

Vale looked at me. He looked so calm, so focused. I

couldn't stand it.

"No," I repeated. "I will. Not. Kneel."

"Jessica—"

"I'd rather die than listen to you," I whispered hoarsely.

"Did you hear what they did to your friend next door?"

I turned my head away. I'd heard April's screams, but I wasn't going to let that affect me.

"I won't do it. I won't."

"He'll do it to you. Unless you obey me."

I shook my head helplessly.

"I don't want to."

"It doesn't matter what you want," he said, more firmly now. "You're one of El Alfa's girls now, and you'll have to obey. We can do this the easy way or the hard way."

El Alfa. I rolled the words in my mouth.

Vale went over to the wall and unhooked the chains, loosening them. My arms dropped as the chains gave some slack. I backed up away from the door until I was almost touching the wall. If he was going to touch me, I was going to give him a fight.

When he turned and saw me crouching back against the wall, there was a strange look in his face. Disappointment, maybe, or sadness. He clasped his hands loosely in front of him and stood in front of me, a mountain of muscle in a business suit. Like a wolf in sheep's clothing.

"El Alfa wants me to teach you how to kneel," he said, slowly, like he was testing the waters.

"Who's El Alfa?"

"He's the man who kidnapped you. He's the one who owns you."

"You're the one who kidnapped me!"

He shrugged, but I could see a flash of anger in his eyes. It made me even madder. How dare he be angry, when he was the one responsible for all this? He stood there so calmly, so controlled. I wanted to push him off the edge.

"I didn't—"

"*You* were the one who lured me out into the alley," I hissed. I set my foot against the wall, coiling up my energy to strike. "*You're* the one who gagged me! You killed James!"

I whipped my arm up to hit him, but he caught me before I could even land a blow. He shoved me back against the wall. I could feel his body pressed up against me.

Before, when we'd been in the club, I'd arched against him, and all those sensations came back with a rush. The scent of his cologne filled my nostrils. I struggled to maintain my anger, to lash out, but I was pinned.

I couldn't imagine why my body would betray me so much as to desire him. I writhed, but it only made the coil inside me tighten. *No.* As much as I hated him, my body didn't listen. I moaned.

"You wanted me before," he whispered in my ear. "Do you want me now?"

"*No.*"

He pulled back, and my body ached hollowly.

"No?"

He was teasing me, I could tell.

"You wanted me at the club. You loved it."

"I didn't know you were a monster."

Instead of being insulted, he looked even calmer. More controlled. It infuriated me even more. I squirmed, but he was holding me too tightly.

"I won't hurt you, but you have to obey me. Otherwise, I can't promise you anything."

"I don't want your promises! You're a goddamn monster!"

"Oh, Jessica—"

He caressed my hair idly. The fury inside of me boiled over. How dare he!

"You killed James!"

Then I was sobbing, beating my fist uselessly at his thick shoulder. "You killed him! You killed him! You—"

"Do you think if I hadn't shot him, he would still be alive?"

I stared baldly into Vale's face. He looked so calm, so impassive.

"What do you mean? You—"

"I pulled the trigger, but it was El Alfa who killed your friend. And he'll kill you too, if you don't behave perfectly."

I gritted my teeth.

"Then shoot me now, and get it over with."

He smiled softly, as though I was kidding.

"That's not what I'm here for."

"What are you here for?"

He looked at me, and for a moment, I saw something slip. His perfect, calm face twisted into an expression that was so pained, it made me ache. Then it disappeared, and his face turned back to ice.

With one motion, he grabbed my dress in his fists and tore. I yelped as his hands ripped at the fabric, my heart pounding against my ribcage. I yanked back at the chains, but the leather cuffs were tight around my wrists. I had nowhere to go. Terror gripped me.

"Don't! Stop! Please—"

The dress was a tangle of fabric at my feet. My bra was bunched up under my breasts from where Mimi had tried to hide the straps, and I was exposed.

I had never been naked in front of a man like this before, and all of my defenses went out the window. I tried to hold onto my anger, but it was quickly disappearing, replaced by fear. I crossed my hands in front of my chest.

"What's that?"

Vale wasn't looking at my breasts. Instead, he stared at the scar across my belly. My fluttering heart skipped another beat.

"What?"

"That scar. What's it from?"

I hadn't thought about my scar in a while. It had been a few years since it had happened, and I wasn't about to tell him the truth.

"I got my appendix out," I said. It was the same lie I told anyone who asked at the beach or swimming pool.

His hand snaked out and touched the white seam. I gasped as he touched my belly, the coil inside of me vibrating with tension. Fear and desire mixed inside of me, turning my stomach. Why? Why was he looking at my scar?

It would make me worth less, I realized, with a leap of breath. The scar that reminded me of my imperfection.

Would he kill me because of it? Was I useless to him now?

But as his fingers slid across the puckered white skin, I saw something else in his eyes. A kind of curiosity. When he looked up at me, though, his eyes turned blank, glassy like the surface of a frozen lake.

"We'll work on kneeling later. Remember, though, that there's no other way out of this. You'll obey me, or you'll die. It's really that simple. Get used to it."

He went to the door and pulled the chains taut. I stumbled forward, my arms stretching up over my head. He wrapped the chains around the hooks once, twice, three times, securely. I was locked in this position.

He came back and reached out toward my chest. I cringed, but he only readjusted the bra back up, covering my breasts.

"Remember that, Jessica," he said. His eyes flickered down over my body, to the white scar on my belly. "And don't lie to me again."

My mouth dropped open, but I couldn't find anything to reply with. Then he turned abruptly and left the room, the iron door clanging shut behind him.

I didn't think I could sleep in that position, with my arms stretched out at either side of my body. But after a while, the ache in my arms grew familiar and exhaustion won out. As I drifted off into unconsciousness, his words rang through my head.

Get used to it.

What other horrors, I wondered, would I have to get used to in here?

Chapter Seventeen

Vale

When I woke up the next day, I was greeted by one of the girls in white gauze. She knelt down in front of me with a lavish breakfast platter of fruit and meats.

I asked to see El Alfa. The girl told me he had left the compound already. I asked where he had gone, but she only shook her head. Nobody knew where he had gone, or when he would get back.

Instead, I went back downstairs to Jessica's room. She looked smaller already, more cowed. When the door clanged shut, she looked up at me with bleary eyes.

I didn't want her to hate me, but how could she not? I was a murderer. A kidnapper. And I had to get her to obey me... or else she would be killed. How could I do it?

"Are you ready to kneel for me?"

"No."

I let her chains loose. She crumpled to the ground, moaning. Immediately, though, she pushed herself up on one knee, then the other. With tremendous effort, she got up on her feet. I could see her legs trembling.

"No."

Her chin jutted out, defiant. She was beautiful, so beautiful. I wanted to know everything about her.

I wanted to know why she'd lied about her scar.

"No? You're not going to obey me?"

"I'll never obey you."

She had to, though. I couldn't explain to her that I

was a good guy. For one, she'd never believe it. For two, it would be a liability. So I had to be the bad guy.

I clenched my jaw. Whatever it took, I decided. Whatever I said to her, however I did it, I would have to get her to obey. I walked around her slowly. She stayed away from me as I circled her, but the chains didn't let her go far.

I took hold of one of them and yanked it, pulling her toward me. She spun away but I gripped her around the waist. Instead of hitting me, though, she froze. I could feel her body shaking under my palm.

"Are you going to hurt me?" she asked hoarsely.

"That's one possibility," I said, keeping my voice cool. I needed to scare her in order to get her to obey. "I've been trained very well in torture."

"And killing," she whispered.

"Yes," I said honestly. "That too."

I could hurt her, or I could scare her. And I didn't want to hurt her.

I pressed my body against her back. She breathed in sharply as I trailed my hand down her side. I was playing a part, but as I touched her I found myself enjoying it.

Did that make me a monster? A real monster? I didn't know. All I knew was that if I couldn't convince her to play my games, she would be under the mercy of El Alfa. And from what I'd seen, he had no mercy to spare.

Tearing her clothes off hadn't convinced her to obey. I had to scare her somehow. If she called my bluffs, I would have to act on my threats. So I would have to be very, very convincing.

My hand came around her waist, gripping her hip loosely. With the other, I pulled a knife from my belt. I'd taken it from my breakfast plate, the only weapon I could find. I hoped it looked scary enough.

"But I don't need a gun to kill. Oh, no. There are many ways to kill, dear."

I slid my hand up under her breast, pressing her back, closer to me. Her heart thudded under my palm. I raised the knife up in front of us, letting it twirl in my fingers. I wasn't lying—I'd learned a fair amount of knifeplay back when I'd been actively working for Uncle Sam. It had always been a favorite of mine, and now it would pay off. With a final flourish, I flipped the knife so that the point was directly in front of her face.

Brave girl, she didn't even flinch back away from the danger. I wouldn't have known her fear except for the heartbeat that quickened under her skin. She couldn't control that.

"You won't kill me," she said, but the last word caught in her throat. "That's not why you brought me here."

"There are a lot of girls in the Tijuana clubs," I said. "If you don't think I can replace you, you're wrong. And if you think you'll stay alive without obeying me, you're wrong." That, at least, was the truth. I had to figure out a way to get her to listen to me, or El Alfa would have at her.

"The easiest way to kill someone," I said, letting the knife drop down to her neck, "is of course, to slit the throat."

I pressed the blade down at the hollow of her neck. She swallowed. I bent my head and kissed the side of her throat, dragging the knife down to her sternum. Her breathing caught as my lips tasted her skin. She was salty, delicious.

I couldn't stop my cock from throbbing hard at the taste of her. No, I wouldn't hold anything back. I didn't need to. She needed to know exactly what would happen to her if she didn't obey. *She needed to be scared.* It was the only way I could make sure she would survive.

"You can also stab someone in the heart. From the front," I said, tapping the tip of the knife on top of her breast, "or the back. You need to be careful, though, or you'll hit the ribcage. A rib can stop a knife, or shatter the blade. So you hold it sideways."

I held the knife up in demonstration. The blade was flat, parallel to the ground.

"This way it's less likely to hit a rib, you understand? It'll slip right in." I whispered the words into her ear as I dropped the knife down.

"You can also stab lower. Here," I said, pressing against her back, "for the kidneys. Slice straight across, and you can empty the guts out of someone. It will still take time to die. Maybe better to put the knife lower, and to the side." I moved the knife across her scar, then further to the right and down. "Where the appendix is."

She swallowed hard but didn't say anything. Did she already know I had caught her in a lie? Probably.

"Then there's the femoral artery. Do you know where that is?"

She shook her head, and my hand moved down. Down past her stomach. With the knife, I caressed her skin, being careful not to cut. The flat of the blade moved against her inner thigh, and she inhaled a sharp breath as I pushed in, applying pressure. Still, she didn't cry out.

"Right here," I said. "You can bleed out in seconds."

I waited, her heartbeat like a dying bird's patter under my hand. She had to know that obedience wasn't optional. But instead of giving in, she squared her shoulders back against my chest. I could feel the heat radiating through my shirt.

"If you're going to kill me, kill me," she said softly.

Disappointment flooded through me. She was stronger than she looked, that was for sure. Without thinking, I bent my head against and kissed her shoulder, inhaling deeply. The faint traces of her perfume wafted into my nostrils and I held her closer.

It was then that she let out a soft cry. I felt her heartbeat jump up a notch, and she twisted in my arms.

That was it.

As soon as I understood what I had to do, I let the knife drop away. The blade clattered on the ground. My hand slid between her thighs and she jerked away from me. Tried to. I had her in my grip, and there was no getting away. When my fingers slid under her panties, I found her already soaking wet.

How hadn't I realized what was happening? Her heartbeat wasn't quickening from fear, as I'd though. It was something else altogether. The discovery shocked me more than I liked to admit. She tried to kick me, but I pulled her up, off the ground a few inches so that she had no leverage.

"Please, no—"

"Oh, darling," I said, feeling sick with what I had to do, but also strangely thrilled. "Darling, darling Jessica. You've been waiting for me to do this for a while, haven't you?"

Chapter Eighteen

Jessica

"No!"

I twisted in his arms, but his hand was still firmly pressed against me down there. I could feel his fingers, slippery with my desire, pushing under my panties.

My body was a traitor. As soon as he'd come around from behind me, I'd felt myself responding to his touch in a way that I never intended.

"Stop," I moaned. But I didn't want him to stop. With one touch, he'd set my nerves on fire. I hated it. I loved it. More than that, I hated that I loved it. There was nothing I could do but writhe in his arms as he gathered me back against his strong chest. My arms were still stretched out, and I had no way to pull his hands off of me.

"It doesn't feel like you want me to stop, Jessica."

He was right. I was soaking wet, and the coil inside of me grew tighter and tighter as his fingers began to stroke me on either side of my slit.

"Please, no…" My voice was hoarser than I remembered, darker.

"Close your eyes," he said, and despite myself, I obeyed him. With my eyes closed, everything seemed to float away. It was all a nightmare. Nothing was real. Nothing except his fingers pressing against my most secret parts, his voice whispering in my ear.

"There's nothing you can do, so why not enjoy it?"

I wanted to rip myself away, but there was nowhere to go. His fingers stroked me, long strokes that sent burning thrills through my core. The coil inside me wound tighter.

"Oh, Jessica," he whispered. "You want this so bad, don't you?"

With his thumb, he flicked my swollen clit. I choked back a cry and arched against him. His hand pressed tight against me under my panties. I shook my head from side to side, my eyes clenched shut. Everything in me was clenched, it seemed. I was on tiptoe, unable to avoid his touch. His fingers probed, exploring, and I gasped in my breaths. The air in the cell was so hot. Stifling hot.

"Please—"

But I didn't know what I was asking him for. I couldn't speak, my mind wasn't coherent, and his strokes began to come faster, with more pressure. The coil wound tight, wound around my chest, around my legs. My arms were stretched taut against the chains and I still didn't open my eyes. I couldn't. His fingers pressed and stroked, avoiding the one spot that ached the worst.

"Beautiful, beautiful Jessica. I want you to obey me, darling."

The throbbing between my thighs was unbearable. Still, I managed to gasp a breath.

"*No.*"

Then his lips touched my neck again. I whipped my head around, but his hand came up around my throat and stopped me from moving. His thumb pressed against my throat, right at the base of my collarbone, as his other thumb ran teasingly around my swollen clit.

He licked me. His tongue was hot against my skin,

the whole room was hot, and I was dizzy beyond anything I'd ever imagined. It wasn't just the air, or the heat. It was the uncontrollable desire that wracked my body that I fought against with every piece of my being.

But my body would not listen. As his thumb circled closer to my aching core, sparks of pure need fired through my system. My body arched, jerking my hips involuntarily as he stroked me. My panties were soaked. My breath came in short gasping bursts. And still he wound the coil inside me tighter and tighter.

"Obey me," he said. He repeated the words over and over, and as he said them, his fingers began to curl into me, stroking at the same rhythm as his words. "*Obey me. Obey me.*"

No.

I could no longer tell if I spoke aloud or just imagined the words. Everything was so hot and I was so, so dizzy. The throbbing need working its way through my body made my mouth dry even as my thighs were soaked wet and slippery.

"*Obey me.*"

His fingers worked me roughly, coiling the loop inside of me tighter and tighter. I swayed into his touch, wanting everything and hating myself for it. I was so close—so close—

Then he pulled his hand back, and I cried out.

He brought his hand up and grasped my chin. My lips parted as his thumb brushed across my bottom lip. I tasted myself, salty and slick on his fingers. Then his tongue pressed against my neck just under my ear, and he sucked hard. Shivers burst through my body and I moaned.

"You want me to touch you again?" he asked. I

couldn't even shake my head at him. His body was against mine, and I could feel his cock on the small of my back, pressing hard. It was the only consolation I had - that no matter how much he made me ache with desire, I was having the same effect on him.

"*Kneel,*" he said.

The rasping sound that tore from my throat wasn't a word. I wrenched away from him, but he only took it as encouragement. With renewed vigor, he thrust his hand between my thighs and forced me open.

"*Please!*"

His hand sawed back and forth slowly, deliberately, dragging skin across skin in a terrible friction that sent me into tremoring shocks. His tongue was on my throat, his teeth gripping my earlobe, his lips hot and wanting.

"Oh, you want this, you beautiful girl. You need it, don't you? Kneel, my darling. Kneel."

The terrible truth was that he was right. I needed what he had to offer, and without another word I let my weight sink against his hand. My hips thrust forward and back, seeking release. The coil inside me was vibrating with tension. I needed release so badly, needed his hand against me. He had pulled me to the brink of ecstasy, and I desperately wanted him to push me over the edge. I let my body fall against his hand, and as I fell forward, he eased me down to my knees. Then, before I could throw myself over the edge into bliss, he yanked his hand away from me.

The sound I made was halfway between a cry and a moan.

"Good girl," he said.

"*No*—" I gasped. The ache inside of me was throbbing so hard I could barely breathe. I needed release.

"You did well," he said, stepping back. His hands left a cold shadow on my skin when they were gone. The floor was cold and hard under my knees. I gulped air, but it was not enough. My legs pressed together and I clenched hard, but the ache inside me did not go away. He had led me to the edge and left me there, dangling. Unfulfilled.

"No," I said dumbly. *"Please…"*

"Do you want me to make you come?"

The words were so blunt that they came like a slap to the face. I would never admit to it. How could I admit that I needed something like that from this monster?

He waited for only a second, and then that slow smile came over his face. His teeth, white and perfect, like the teeth of the Cheshire Cat shining out of the darkness.

As he stepped over my chains in front of me, his icy blue stare made me shiver. His face was calmly amused. He had been using me, manipulating me. I couldn't stand it.

"Fuck you," I seethed. All of my need turned into bright anger. "Fuck you, you bastard!"

His smile turned into a low laugh. He knelt down then in front of me, so that we were face to face. He caressed my cheek with one hand. I pulled away from him, and he let me go, still laughing.

"You need me, darling," he said. "You don't know how much you need me. Next time, you kneel right away. Then I'll give you what you want."

"I don't—I don't want—"

"Of course you don't want it. You hate me. Is that it?"

I stared up at him dizzily. Blinding hate, yes. That's what this was. Nothing else. How could he be anything other than a monster?

"Listen, darling. Listen to me."

His hand grasped my chin and he forced me to look at him. I gritted my teeth. The morning sun was shining in his eyes. The light seemed to pierce through the irises all the way to the bottom, reflecting the clearest, purest blue. It was the blue of the sky. In that instant, I wondered if I would ever see sky again.

He seemed to read my thoughts. His hand softened under my chin, stroking my jawline.

"There's no way out but through me. Give me what I need, and I'll give you what you need. Even if you hate what you need. I'm not here to judge you."

My mouth opened, but no words came. He had no idea what he'd said to me, how it would affect me. Tears suddenly stung the backs of my eyes.

There was such gentleness to him, a kind of gentleness that I'd never gotten from anyone. Not from my friends, not from my parents. Not from myself.

I'm not here to judge you.

Then there was a moment between us that made me think that something else was going on, something behind the scenes. A tension in the air, as though he was reaching out to me and hoping that I would see it, invisible though it was. The space between us crackled with unspoken words. And the thought came to mind unbidden: *He's not a monster.*

He stood abruptly, as if he'd said too much. The chains rattled, and my arms were pulled taut. I did not even look to see him leave. When the iron door slammed shut, I was already crying.

Chapter Nineteen

Vale

That morning had taken all of the energy out of me and left me hollow. Jessica had knelt, finally.

Instead of being satisfied, though, I was intensely disturbed. Disturbed that she had so much power over my emotions. Disturbed that she seemed to want me, even after everything I had done.

I'd gone back to my room and jerked off in the shower, and afterwards I hated myself more than ever. I was torturing the poor girl, using her feelings for me against her. She had tried so hard to resist, but I'd broken her down. She was right. I was a monster.

But I was a monster who was going to complete this mission, no matter what I had to do.

I spent the day exploring El Alfa's compound to scout out the layout of the house. I expected to be stopped by the guards, but none of them seemed to even notice me. I supposed that by killing the boy, I had gained the trust of everyone in El Alfa's circle. The realization didn't stop the darkness from winding around my heart, though.

El Alfa himself didn't reappear until that evening. David, who I guessed was his main henchman, called me into dinner at five o'clock and led me to a grand dining hall.

A long oak table stretched down the room under the vaulted ceiling. There were a few men already seated at the table, mostly Mexicans, all in business suits. Behind them, a column of girls stood at attention. One of them stepped forward at the lift of a hand to pour more wine into a businessman's glass.

El Alfa sat at the head of the table, and there was an empty seat right next to him. As I came closer, I realized that Valentina was there, on the floor. Kneeling.

I sat down, being careful not to hit her with the chair as I pulled it out. Two of the other girls came forward. One of them pushed my chair back in as I sat. The other shook out a cream-colored cloth napkin and laid it on my lap. Then they both stepped away, and the girl with the urn of wine came forward to pour for me.

Throughout all of this, Valentine never moved once. Her hands were stretched in front of her, palms up. Her forehead hovered just above the floor. And despite all of the feet around her, she stayed perfectly still.

"Welcome, my friend," El Alfa said. "Did you sleep well last night?"

"Fine," I said.

"You must have been desperate to want to work for me."

"Not at all."

"No?"

"I enjoy this kind of work," I lied.

"Killing?"

My eyes flicked up to the camera mounted to the wall. I wanted El Alfa to think he had me running scared. I pretended to be nervous as I picked up my glass of wine and took a gulp.

"No," I said, after a moment of fake hesitation. "I enjoy training."

"Excellent. Let's see how you did with the girl."

"The girl?"

I jerked my head up from my wineglass.

"She's not ready yet," I said.

Not ready? That was an understatement if I'd ever made one. If El Alfa went to go see Jessica, she'd be just as likely to spit in his face as to kneel.

"Still," El Alfa said smoothly. "We must see some progress."

He snapped his finger, and David left the dining hall, a sick smile on his face. I composed my face in a neutral expression, even as worry surged up in my throat. If he saw how disobedient Jessica was, he would surely torture her.

Why did I care? I was here for one reason only: to get close to El Alfa so I could kill him. The girl meant nothing to me.

That's not true.

Why? Why was I so worried for her? It was her fault if she got hurt, wasn't it? And yet, as we waited for the henchman to bring her up, I felt panic begin to creep in at the edges. I fought the emotion. Breathe in, breathe out. Control. Why was it so hard?

Because you chose her.

It wasn't my fault, not at all. And yet I felt a stupidly strong sense of possession. I'd picked her, and now she was here, and I was responsible for her. When the door opened and the henchman came in, pulling her by her cuffs, I couldn't help but swallow back a lump of anger in my throat. Her lip was bleeding. It was a fresh wound. I looked at David as he jerked her to El Alfa's side, where Valentina was still poised on the floor, but he didn't meet my eyes.

"Kneel," El Alfa said.

For one terrible moment, I thought she wasn't going to do it. She caught my eye, and I felt a surge of panic break through my control. For a split second only. My fist clenched my glass of wine, and I thought that she would be killed right then and there.

But no. She sank down almost immediately to her knees, falling down hard onto the floor. And—God bless her—I hadn't taught her anything else, but she copied Valentina nearly perfectly. Her hands came out in front of her, palms up. Her head was bent to the ground.

I breathed a sigh of relief.

"You've done well," El Alfa said. "Quick work. Not perfect, but that will come."

He licked his bottom lip.

"Stand, girl," he said. As quick as she had knelt, Jessica stood up. Her face was blank. Her eyes stared straight ahead. The cut on her lip dripped a trickle of blood down her chin, but she made no effort to wipe it off. El Alfa frowned.

"Why is she cut?"

David shifted his weight from one foot to another. But El Alfa was speaking to me.

"I don't like it when their faces are ruined. It makes them less valuable. I told you this. You cut her—"

"I didn't."

El Alfa wasn't used to being interrupted. His eyes flashed darkly.

"Excuse me," I said, apologizing with my tone as well as my words. "David must have misunderstood your orders. She was not cut this morning when I left her."

I let a hint of irritation come into my voice.

"I thought you said she was mine."

With that last sentence, I clasped my hands together. Obediently. I was the good one, the obedient one.

El Alfa looked over to David, who shifted his weight back again. When he spoke, his voice was a stammer.

"I didn't mean to. You— you understand," David said. "When I went down to get her, she didn't—she was very uncooperative. There wasn't any other way."

El Alfa glanced over at Jessica, standing still next to the table. Her eyes were fixed ahead onto the wall.

"She looks quite cooperative to me," he said drily.

"But—"

"Do you disagree?"

El Alfa waited for David's response, the chicken bone held tensely in his fingers. He bent the bone suddenly with his thumb, so hard that the bone cracked and splintered. David's shoulders jerked back.

"No, of course not, El Alfa."

El Alfa turned back to me. His face was hard set.

"She is yours," he said, looking up an inch or so into my eyes. "You are her master... for now. Do you think you can continue to train her?"

I nodded once, my hands still clasped.

"Yes."

El Alfa dropped the cracked chicken bones back onto his plate. They landed with a dull clank on the porcelain.

"Then you have her. Nobody else will interfere. If they do, you have my permission to punish them as well."

David bristled but said nothing.

"Make sure she learns to kneel softly. I don't want her bruising."

"Yes, sir," I said.

"And David," he said, his voice dropping in tone, "don't touch the girl."

"Yes, sir," he repeated through gritted teeth.

I let my hands unclasp and stretched my fingers out to relax them.

As frightened as I was for Jessica, I felt some measure of relief that El Alfa wouldn't let his henchmen hurt her any more. If I was in charge, I could get her to obey me.

I could find a way to control her.

I knew it.

Chapter Twenty

Jessica

I stumbled back to the cell in front of the guard who had hurt me, my knees hurting from kneeling down on the hard ground. But nothing hurt as badly as the ache between my legs. Vale had left me unfulfilled.

Now I was hungry and thirsty, *and* unsatisfied. The first two I could bear. But Vale had tried to take away my dignity by making me beg for him.

"April?" I whispered. I couldn't hear her from the cell next door, and the door had been closed when I'd gone by. "April?"

There was no response. I called louder, my voice rising to a yell.

"*April!*"

The door of my cell opened with a clang and I jumped back. My chains rattled against the stone walls on either side of me.

It was Vale. He had a plate in his hands.

"You shouldn't yell," he said. Immediately I shrunk even further into myself. His voice, admonishing, reminded me of my mother. Always scolding. I gritted my teeth before speaking.

"My… my friend. The one in the cell next door. Is she okay?"

Vale stared at me strangely. His voice when he spoke next was softer than before.

"Here. Eat this." He held out a piece of bread from

off of the plate. I only stared at it, unable to think coherently. My stomach growled.

"Please," I insisted. "Her name is April. Is she alright?"

The softness disappeared as quickly as it had appeared. Vale's face was, once again, ice.

"Listen to me, darling. In here, you shouldn't worry about anyone other than yourself. Understood? She's dead, as far as you know."

I flinched at the word. I couldn't believe something like that, not in here. April wasn't dead, any more than I was. She was fine. *We would both be fine.*

"At least drink something, will you?"

I hadn't realized that he was offering a cup of water. He lifted the cup to my lips and it was like a spell was broken. Thirst came clawing back up my throat and all I could think about was the physical pain that I'd endured.

I gulped at the lip of the cup, dribbling water down my almost-naked body. When he pushed the bread at me again, I bit into it. Hunger woke up my system and I gnawed at the piece of bread. Right then, it was the most delicious thing I'd ever tasted.

"Here," he said. He ripped off a small piece of bread for me so that I wouldn't have to tear it myself with my teeth. When I took it, my lips brushed his fingers, and he inhaled shallowly.

There it was—that crackling electricity in the air again. Something between us that I couldn't name or put my finger on. A connection that seemed to break through the icy wall he kept in front of him.

He pulled back and wiped his fingers on his shirt absentmindedly. It was something he was staying away from, I understood just then. I didn't know why. But I knew that of all the guards in here, he was different.

Was I going crazy? I'd heard about women who fell in love with their kidnappers, but I'd never thought that anything so ridiculous would happen to me. It wasn't that he had brought me here, though. That wasn't why my body ached every time he so much as grazed me with his palm. It was something else, something deeper. A secret that I could sense beneath his surface. A secret that he didn't want me to get at.

"You still have blood on your lip," he said.

I tilted my head up and spoke with a hint of sarcasm.

"Untie me and I'll wipe it off."

Instead, Vale grabbed my chin and kissed me. His lips took my bottom lip and sucked. He sucked soft at first, then hard, sucked at the cut El Alfa's henchman had made. Pain sparked through my body, pain and desire both.

And for a moment, a horrible, horrible moment, I couldn't stop myself from kissing him back.

I pushed forward on my tiptoes to deepen the kiss, and he pushed back, conquering me with his mouth. He licked my bottom lip, sucked at it, until I could taste the coppery blood. I moaned, and my body arched into him, stopping only when the chains at my wrists tightened and held me back.

Vale looked down at me in wonder. The electrical energy between us seemed to brighten the room, even as my shadow passed over his body.

"Jessica," he whispered.

I closed my eyes. I would not give him the satisfaction of letting him see what he had done to me. It was crazy, this blistering attraction. But nobody could blame me for going crazy. Was I crazy?

His hand slid between my legs, stroking me, and despite myself I turned wet as soon as he touched me. I was crazy. I was. This was all insane.

"Vale—" I started to say. I was choking on the air in this stone cell.

"Don't lie to me, Jessica," he whispered. "Do you want it?"

"Vale, please—" My words fluttered out over my tongue, but I didn't know what to say. I wanted him, yes, I was crazy and I wanted him and my world was crumbling down all around me because of it.

"You want me. I know you want me."

"No."

Had I said the word, or had it died on my tongue? His hand burned the place between my thighs, coiling me tighter with every slow stroke.

"Tell me you want me to fuck you."

His voice was a growl that sent shudders down my body. I couldn't do this. Even though every dream of mine had been about this—or something like this—it wasn't right. There was something that kept us apart, and I couldn't bring myself to let go completely. I wasn't this girl. Jessica was a good girl.

"No," I said weakly. "Please—"

"You're so fucking hot for me. Look at you, your perfect tight hot cunt. You're so wet—"

My breath was hot in my throat, and every part of me tensed as his fingers stroked me. His body was strong, but as much as I wanted him to possess me, I knew that I couldn't do this. Not really.

"Please… please…oh!!"

He flicked my clit, and I was there already, the coil inside me wound so tight that all it would take was a little more.

"I'll make it good for you," he said. "Christ, I'll make you come hard all over my cock, I swear it."

The worst thing was that I wanted it. I was scared, terrified, but I wanted it so bad.

"Tell me how you like it. Tell me how you want me to fuck you."

"No," I said, dizziness overtaking my brain. "I don't—"

"Tell me," he said. He whispered. He growled. "Tell me."

"Tell you?"

My voice was a breath that was so light, it floated away. His hands were the only things keeping me anchored to the ground.

"Tell me how you like being fucked."

I bit my lip, shook my head. Even now, I couldn't lie to him. How could I answer that? I didn't know how I liked being fucked. I'd never been fucked. In that instant, I wanted to be fucked, though. It would be a lie if I denied it. I wanted him to fuck me so badly.

"I don't—I don't—"

"Tell me."

I said the only thing I could say.

"I'm a virgin."

Vale yanked back like he had touched a hot flame, ripping his hands away from me. Immediately the need inside my core flamed up. But the ache in my body from being left untouched wasn't nearly as terrifying as the look he gave me. He stared at me so coldly that it seemed all of the heat in the air disappeared. It was like he was going to rip my head off right then and there.

"Vale?" My voice was hoarse. I knew that there was more to him, a secret that I hadn't quite been able to catch. Now, though, he pulled back from me and I felt alone, completely alone. And terrified. The walls of the room seemed to close in on me. What had I done?

"Vale?"

He didn't say anything, only giving me that terrible, conflicted look. Then he turned and left, slamming the door behind him.

"Vale!"

Fear choked my throat. I immediately regretted telling him that I'd never been with a man before. Stories of virgins poured into my mind unbidden.

Virgin sacrifices. Virgin blood. Stories of terrible men who pay top price to torture and fuck virgins.

God, I shouldn't have told him. He'd come back with that awful man, El Alfa, and do terrible things. They would sell me to the highest bidder, to a man who wanted to take a girl's virginity. Jesus, what would they do to me?

I breathed shallowly, panting for oxygen. The collar around my throat seemed unbearably tight. And I couldn't turn around. I couldn't go *anywhere*. Blood rushed in my ears and dizziness began to overtake me.

I'd only ever fainted once before, when I was a kid and overheated on the playground. But the panic that rose up inside of me was enough to make it happen again. Black spots shimmered in my vision and I gasped for breath.

As I blacked out, I saw the shadow from the moon behind me. It was a cold, cold blue shadow, colder even than Vale's eyes, and I could only whisper April's name as I fell into the shadow.

Chapter Twenty-One

Vale

I'd thought she—fuck, I'd thought she _wanted_ me. I'd thought that there was something between us, but of course there wasn't. There couldn't be. I had kidnapped her.

Now I couldn't get her face out of my mind. That face she'd made when I asked her how she wanted me to fuck her. I'd made the biggest mistake.

"Please, no," she'd said, and I hadn't believed it, but I sure as hell believed it now. What had I done? What had I become?

Ten's voice rang through my head—"You'll be doing his dirty work."

Nothing was as dirty as my own dark thoughts. A virgin, and I wanted to fuck her, for Chrissakes, and she was a virgin and I had chosen to throw her into this hellhole. No matter what El Alfa had told me to do, there was no way that this was going to be a part of training. I couldn't do it.

I'd thought she wanted me, I thought I'd seen that in her face, and then it was gone and I was just a monster again.

No. No. I couldn't do this—I just couldn't.

I leaned over the toilet in my bathroom and retched. Nothing came up but air, but I retched again and again, thinking about what I'd almost done to someone who was completely innocent.

"You alright?"

My head snapped up. David leaned against the doorframe. El Alfa's head honcho. The man responsible for Jessica's cut lip. I'd tasted blood when I kissed her, but now I tasted blood again. I couldn't wait for the chance to kill El Alfa, and I hoped to whatever God existed that I had the chance to kill David when that time came.

"Why are you in my room?" I asked, standing up and letting my body draw itself up into its full height. I was a head taller than this asshole, but he was a whole lot meaner. He scowled.

"I heard you in here and thought I'd make sure you were okay."

Sure you did.

"I'm fine."

"You were vomiting." He picked at his chin, where his sunburn was peeling right under his jawline.

"Must have been something I ate for dinner," I said nonchalantly. I rinsed my hands in the sink and splashed water on my face. Still he stood in the doorway, watching me with that ugly look on his face. Dark eyebrows that ripped across his forehead. A mean look, like a dog who couldn't wait to bite.

"Can I help you with anything?" I asked, turning around and crossing my arms. He might have been head guard to El Alfa, but I was here now, and he wasn't going to bully me around. I wasn't going to let him.

"Yeah, maybe," he said, smiling sickly.

"What?"

"How's training going?"

I thought of Jessica's split lip, and how she had recoiled from my touch when I'd asked her if she wanted me to fuck her. Was I any better than this asshole? Maybe not. But I sure as hell was going to try to keep her from harm.

"Fine," I said coldly.

"If you ever get sick of training that girl, you just let me know."

He leered at me, and something inside me broke. Despite myself, I couldn't hold back the barb.

"Yeah?" I said. "Does El Alfa let his dog train bitches?"

Maybe I wasn't in control of myself, but damn, it felt good.

Red with anger, David jumped forward at me. He lifted his arm with a punch that was telegraphed so far ahead, it was nothing for me to catch him by the wrist.

I slammed him into the bathroom wall, holding him up just high enough that he was forced to stand on tiptoe. My arm braced against his neck, threatening the chokehold I could easily put him into.

"Let me go!" he hissed.

"Sure," I said. "As soon as you apologize for trying to hit me."

"I wasn't—wasn't gonna hit you—I'm not…"

He squirmed, but that was as much apology as I was likely to get from him. I let him down, shoving him towards the doorway. He caught himself on the doorframe and craned his head back at me when he was just out of arm's reach.

"You're fucking with the wrong guy," he said.

David stormed off and I slumped back against the sink. This wasn't working. I had to kill El Alfa. I had to kill him soon. But the raid wouldn't be for another week.

That was a week I had to spend training Jessica. A week I had to spend sparring with David. A week to keep my secret hidden from El Alfa.

Back at home, it had seemed doable. Easy, even. Now, though, I was wondering if I would survive until then.

I woke up in the morning half hungover. I'd drunk half the bottle of whiskey I'd found in the bar cabinet in my room. The sun was blinding.

After a quick shower, I went down to the cells with a bottle of water and the plate of breakfast that the servants had left for me. Jessica would need it. She hadn't been able to eat much the last time I'd seen her, but she would waste away to nothing if I didn't encourage her to eat when she could.

I would be gentle, I thought to myself. I would hold back. No training today, nothing at all. I would let her have a little bit of peace.

But when I got down there, David was standing outside of Jessica's cell. Of all people, this guy.

"I told you to leave her alone—" I started to say.

"El Alfa is inside now," David said, grinning at me. "He's trying her out."

My heart sank as I heard Jessica inside, crying. I put my hand on the door handle, but David leaned his palm against the door, blocking my way. It took every ounce of self-control not to shove him up against the wall again.

"El Alfa doesn't want to be disturbed when he's

visiting with the girls," David said, his evil leer glowing at me in the dim hallway. "But don't worry. He won't leave any permanent damage."

There was nothing I could do but wait. I heard Jessica's muffled cries, and anger swirled up in my body. The darkness swirled up too, unbidden, and it immediately started looking for ways to kill. I could do it now, I thought. It was early, but I could do it. Sure, there were guards at either end of the hall, but if I could overpower David—

The door opened before I could act.

El Alfa stepped out, zipping up his pants. Inside, I saw a glimpse of Jessica, her head bent, sobbing. My body wrenched at the sight, but I controlled it. Control. I had to keep in control.

El Alfa winked at me as he came out into the hallway.

"Train her to suck dick," he said. "She is terrible."

I found that my fists were clenched at my side. But David had a gun, and I'd stupidly come downstairs with nothing, not even the knife from my breakfast plate. Still, the thought echoed through my mind:

Kill him. Kill him. Kill him.

"Hello? You understand, American boy?"

"Yes," I said, controlling the rage in my voice. "I understand. I'll train her."

"Train her today. Make her good. I'll be back later to check."

Kill him. Kill him. Kill him.

But El Alfa was already walking down the hall. David was at his side, his hand on his gun as he looked back over his shoulder at me. I couldn't do anything. I couldn't do a single goddamn thing except for what he had ordered me to do.

First Ten, and now El Alfa. I was made to follow orders, but this was the first time I considered breaking them. Jessica was still crying when I came into the cell with a plate of breakfast that I knew she wouldn't be able to eat.

I had to do this. So did she.

And after today, I don't know if she would hate me more than I already hated myself.

Chapter Twenty-Two

**Jessica**

I was crying when Vale came into my cell. I jerked back as his hand touched my shoulder.

There was vomit on my chin, a little bit of it. El Alfa had gagged me with his ugly cock. I didn't know what to do, and it had been too much. He'd slapped me, and my cheek still ached from the slap. My jaw ached from where he had forced it open. And the rest—I didn't want to remember it. I couldn't.

Vale had a soft look on his face. I didn't know why— I had heard what El Alfa had told him. But he leaned forward with a plate of food.

"Can you eat?" he asked. I shook my head, tears burning my eyes. My stomach was roiling, and even the thought of putting something in my mouth made me gag a little.

He put the plate down and turned to me. His shoulders squared back like a soldier's.

"We're starting new training today," Vale said. "You understand?"

The fear inside me burst out in a flurry of words and tears alternating with each other.

"Please," I said. "I—I can't. I can't do it. I tried. I tried so hard, but I couldn't do it—"

I fell into sobs, trying to hold them back and failing. El Alfa had hit me for crying. I didn't want to be hit again.

"It's alright. I'll teach you."

He closed the door behind him and locked it. Fear seeped in through my body. Not again. Not again.

"Please, no—"

Not again.

"You have to learn," he said firmly. "Did he hurt you?"

I nodded silently.

"Then he'll hurt you again. He'll kill you. Unless you learn."

"I don't think I can." The tears were hot on my cheeks. But Vale didn't look like he was going to hit me, thank God.

"I think you can."

"No—"

"We'll go slowly."

I bit back a sob. This wasn't happening to me. It couldn't be. I felt two strong hands on my shoulders and looked up into Vale's ice-blue eyes. Strangely enough, they had softened again. He was letting the mask slip, or pretending to. He almost seemed compassionate.

"This won't be easy, Jessica," he said. "But you're brave. You can do this. I won't hurt you."

I didn't believe him, although I yearned to. My whole body shook in terror. Then he stepped back and his hands were gone.

I looked up. He was unbuttoning his shirt. My heart began to pound. Why was he getting undressed?

I watched mutely as he pulled his shirt off, my breath drawn away from me by the awful sight. There was a huge scar that ran down his chest from his collarbone all the way down to his stomach. It ended just above the bellybutton.

Tiny scars, too, scars that crisscrossed his biceps and covered his sculpted pecs. Puckers of white flesh.

Vale paused for a moment before taking off his pants. More of them, white lines and seams like he'd let someone draw all over him. He stood there, with only his black briefs covering him. His scars gleamed in the morning light.

I couldn't help but stare, aghast at the scars. How deep they were, how many of them they were.

"What happened to you?" I asked.

He smiled wryly at me.

"I got my appendix out."

I shook my head.

"Really, what happened? You have—God, you have so many of them."

"Are you asking so that you don't have to train?"

I clamped my lips shut and turned my head away. Training. Right. That was why he had come down here. Panic began to rise in my throat again.

"It's alright," he said, and although it wasn't alright, it was *really fucking far from alright*, I started to panic a little less. "I'll tell you, then we can start. I know this is hard for you."

You don't know anything, I wanted to say. But the scars on his chest, the healed tissue, made me question if that was really true. He looked at me like he could read the questions in my mind.

"Most of these are scars from my assignments. I do dangerous work, you know."

I gulped. His hand was tracing the long line of the biggest scar, the one that ran down his whole chest.

"But this one... this one was from my last girlfriend."

I eyed him in disbelief. I didn't know what was weirder, the fact that he was telling me this, or the fact that Vale had dated a girl before. I couldn't imagine him taking a girl out.

"Your girlfriend?"

"She wanted to kill me."

"Why?"

Vale smiled, and it was the coldest smile I'd ever seen. Behind that mirthless expression, I saw the thing he had been hiding from me this whole time. A deep sorrow. It touched his eyes, drew the corners of his mouth down. I could see him struggling to contain the sorrow.

"She was sent to kill me," he said.

"What was her name?"

"Jen."

"How... how did she..."

I didn't know how to ask it, but I didn't have to. Vale understood what I was trying to get at.

"When you trust someone, they can do anything to you. They can hurt you. They can hurt you really bad."

He looked up at me, his face now plainly marked with sorrow. And despite myself, I was curious... curious enough not to worry about making him upset with me. For some reason, standing here in chains in front of the man who had kidnapped me, I felt utterly safe.

"Tell me what happened," I said.

Chapter Twenty-Three

Vale

I stared down at Jessica. I'd thought that she might react differently if I showed her my scars, but now I wasn't sure if I could handle her questions. There was an innocent sincerity in her voice when she asked me what had happened. Like she really wanted to know.

Like she cared about me.

Of course, that couldn't be it. I shook the thought away and went back in my mind to Jen, the one who was responsible for the white bolt of scar tissue going down my sternum.

"I loved her," I said. "At least, I thought I loved her. I thought she loved me, too. She convinced me that what happened between us… was real. I let her in. I told her everything. I was trying to get out of doing—well, this kind of work. I wanted to clean up for her. Get straight, you know. Stop all the bullshit."

I waved my hand around, as though to indicate that all this was just bullshit.

"I bought her a ring. How stupid can you get, right? I was going to propose to her. And we were together that evening, and she took off all my clothes, and slept with me. And before I could pull the ring out of my pants, she'd pulled a knife."

Jessica's eyes went wide.

"But… but you're so big. How could she…"

"How could she attack me, you mean? Yeah, well,

that's the thing about trust. We were big into bondage."

Jessica's eyes, already wide, seemed to pop out of her head. I could see the mental image she had of me, but I had already told her part of the story. I might as well tell her all of it.

"I was—uh, a little tied up when she pulled the knife."

"But... but you got away, though."

"Yeah. Barely. She stabbed me in the wrong spot." I touched the place where the scar started. "Hit my sternum. Bone stopped the tip. Dragged the knife down. Down my chest. I was so surprised, it took a few seconds before I even reacted."

"What did you do?"

She was staring at me with a strange mix of curiosity and horror in her face. At least she wasn't thinking about El Alfa anymore. I was good at telling stories that take your mind off of things.

"Right away I kicked out hard, broke her arm. She dropped the knife, and I snapped the chain tying me to the bed. I mean, it wasn't a real chain, you know, not like these. It was just for fun. My hands were still cuffed when I caught up to her, though, and the cuffs were real enough. I put the cuffs around her neck, and—"

I broke off. Thinking about Jen made goosebumps stand up on my arms.

"You killed her."

I nodded.

"I could feel her heart slowing down as I choked her. The woman I loved. The woman I wanted to spend my life with."

As I spoke to Jessica, I felt myself slipping back into

the past. I could see Jen like she was right there in front of me again. Her face had turned red, then blue. Her lips had gone pale.

I'd killed her. Killed her, killed her, killed her. That's all I was. A killer.

I felt myself starting to lose control. I felt the darkness curling up inside of me. I blinked hard, getting away from the past. I was back in El Alfa's hell, but at least it was a different kind of hell than the one in my mind.

"She was the only person I ever trusted. And the last."

Jessica was quiet. She didn't look scared anymore, only sad. And there was a mark of pity in her face that I didn't want to see. I didn't deserve her pity. I didn't deserve pity from anyone. I was a murderer, and if I'd been tricked by another assassin, then it was my own damn fault.

I turned back to the matter at hand, even though I knew I'd be pushing Jessica away.

"Did El Alfa... did he fuck you?" I asked. I was almost scared to hear the answer to that question, but I had to ask.

She shook her head no, and relief flooded my system.

I went over to the chains and loosened them. Her arms dropped down to her sides. She looked defeated already. I swallowed the lump in my throat. I had to do this. As much as I was afraid to hurt her, I had to act like I was her trainer, her master.

When I pulled down my briefs, though, her eyes widened in fear. I stepped out of them, completely naked. I looked down. The scar ended only a couple of inches above my cock. I wondered if I would be able to get

135

aroused after all that. Shit.

"Tell me what he asked you to do," I said. If El Alfa wanted me to train her, I would train her in exactly the way he wanted.

"He t—told me to suck it. I—I tried. I can't."

"You have to."

Her eyes flashed angrily up at me.

"Is that why you said all this? To get my sympathy before you do the exact same thing to me that he did?"

"No."

"Good cop, bad cop, right?"

I shook my head. There wasn't anything I could do to make this right. I would just have to do it, and get it done with. I only hoped—and this was a stupid hope, a desperate hope—that she wouldn't hate me when it was over.

"No," I said, stepping forward in front of her. "There are no good cops in here. I'm sorry."

Chapter Twenty-Four

Jessica

"Take it in your hand."

I stared at his cock. It hung slightly to one side. Already, it seemed huge, and he wasn't even erect. Fear bolted through my heart.

"I already told you," I said, tears threatening to choke my throat again. "I can't."

"Take it," he said. "Just hold it."

I touched it with my hand. The skin was silky smooth. As I held it, it twitched in my palm.

"Jessica—"

I tilted my chin up. Vale was looking down at me with a look of tenderness in his face. I hated him, God knows I hated him, but there was something else in the way he looked at me that made me feel a little less scared.

"We'll go slow. Okay?"

"Okay," I said, in a voice so small I couldn't believe it belonged to me. My whole body was tense.

"Take your time."

I bit my bottom lip and heard him draw a breath. His cock swelled in my hand.

"Just like that," he said.

"Like what?"

"Your lip… when you bite it like that. Lick it."

I licked my lips experimentally. Vale's cock throbbed, stiffening.

"You're—Christ, you're gorgeous."

I didn't know why he was saying this. El Alfa hadn't said anything at all. He'd just come in and—no. I blinked away the image. That man wasn't here anymore. Instead, it was Vale, Vale with his ice blue eyes and muscles as hard and sculpted as ice, and white scars all over his body, God, they were everywhere.

He's no better.

Intellectually I knew that he was as bad as El Alfa. That this kind of treatment wasn't about him being kind to me. It was about him manipulating me. I struggled to resist my attraction as he stroked my hair back as gently as if he was my boyfriend.

He wasn't kind. He wasn't good. And yet, when his fingers stroked through my hair, my scalp sent tingles straight down through my spine.

"Your hair is so soft," he murmured. "So beautiful."

I couldn't understand why he would try to ply me with compliments. It wasn't as though I could argue with him about any of this. I'd tried to stop El Alfa, and it hadn't worked.

I was terrified that I wouldn't be able to do this, that I would do it all wrong. And then Vale might kill me.

The way he'd killed his last girlfriend.

"Please don't." I turned my head down, breathing out a tremble. His cock was hard in my hand, hot and throbbing. It was so big that I didn't know how I could manage. It would be worse than El Alfa if he tried to make me take it in my mouth. Tears stung my face, burning in the back of my nose and eyes.

"Sorry," he said. He paused to swallow, shifting his weight back. "I can... we can do this later. If you need time."

I blinked back the tears, anger welling up to replace my self-pity. His fake concern was worse than if he had just done it.

"No," I said bluntly. I wanted to get it over with.

He nodded solemnly. His hand cupped my chin and drew me forward. My fingers were loose around his cock. It was hard now, standing erect in front of my face.

"Kiss it," he said. "Wet your lips and kiss it."

I licked my lips. As I did, I felt his whole cock jump in my hand. A strange jolt of pleasure went through me. I could control him.

With only a lick of the lips, I could control him.

I tried it again, and again his cock twitched. And again, the strange burst of pleasure that I could do this.

"Jessica—" he murmured.

I leaned forward and pressed my lips against the tip. The skin was like silk stretched taut, and there was a drop of wetness at the slit. It was sticky against my lips. As I pressed my lips to the hot skin, I could feel the throb of his heartbeat through his cock.

I squeezed the hard length slightly with my hand, testing his cock like it was an animal I was meeting for the first time. A stranger. The vein under my palm beat quickly and I felt my own heartbeat begin to quicken. And how strange it was, to control him with such a little change in pressure.

"Now slide your lips over it." His voice was a low rumble, rasping in the air. "Just the tip."

I followed his instructions, but all of my attention was on the throb of his heart coming through my hand. I began to probe with my tongue, seeing what I could do.

With each touch of my tongue, I found the secret

places that made his heartbeat quicken. The coil inside of me tightened. Feeling him enjoy what I was doing—it was as though I was experiencing it myself. I felt part of me loosen inside as he gasped with pleasure. His eyes were closed when I looked up, and he was biting his lip, and the image tore at me. I shouldn't have been enjoying this, but I was.

"Swirl your tongue around. That's right. All around the ridge of the tip. The most sensitive spot is right underneath on the ridge. If you—ahh!"

He reached forward to brace his hand against the wall. One of his legs was trembling. I could see the muscle in his thigh spasming.

"*Fuck.*"

The word came out loud, echoing in the small cell. He swallowed hard, the sound audible in the small stone cell. I froze, unsure if I had done something wrong.

"Oh, don't stop. Don't—*fuck*, you feel amazing."

There was sweat on his brow and he was still bracing himself with one strong arm over my head.

I touched my tongue again to the spot I'd found, and he groaned again. Again, too, the heat inside me blossomed. I could do this to him.

I was in control.

"*Ohhh.*"

His hips were beginning to twitch, thrusting his cock back and forth. I slid my mouth farther over his shaft with each stroke. At the tip, I would make sure to push against that spot I'd found. His cock was slick with my saliva now, and it slid through my hand even as I gripped it tighter.

"*Fuck yes. Yes. Oh God, yes!*"

I matched his rhythm, feeling his heart beat faster and

faster. My own ache clenched deep inside of me. As much as I tried to shut down the thing inside of me that liked this feeling, I couldn't. I loved the sensation of his heartbeat in my hand. I loved the smooth skin, his cock swollen hard with desire. I had created that desire.

Suddenly he stopped rocking his hips into me. Not wanting to stop, I slid my mouth forward and took him as far as I could into my mouth. My lips wrapped tight around him. I felt his hand on my shoulder.

"Oh Christ, Jessica, I'm going to come—"

His cock went rock hard and I felt the spasm come through my hand as I slid back. With my tongue, I flicked the spot just under his tip. There was no time for more before he exploded inside of my mouth.

By instinct, I swallowed, my lips still around his throbbing head. He shuddered, his hand softening its grip on my shoulder. He let out a gasp of air, and I felt him jerk again in my hand. A shiver went through him, and the shiver thrilled through my body as well.

"God, that was incredible."

I sat back against the floor, astonished at what I'd done. This...this wasn't me.

"Jessica—"

I'd done it. I'd liked doing it. And if he was a monster, then what did that make me?

"Jessica, come here—"

He was pulling me up, and I let him. My legs trembled as I stood, and I felt again the immense ache inside of me, the coil stretched tight. I stood up between him and the wall, the chains clinking at my sides. In the morning sunlight I saw his eyes shining bright like the sky.

Then he bent his head and kissed me.

Chapter Twenty-Five

Vale

I lost control. There was no getting around it. It had only taken what, five minutes? Ten? Her lips on my cock had turned off any rational side of my mind.

I couldn't even pull out in time. She'd been perfect, so goddamn perfect. And then she'd stayed there, sucking the last of my come as I tried not to slam my hips into her while I orgasmed.

So when I pulled her up from the ground, there was nothing I wanted more than to kiss her. My lips pressed against hers, hot and wanting. I'd thrust my tongue against her bottom lip, sucking and biting, and she moaned a small, needy moan that made my cock throb again right away.

"Jessica—"

I kissed her again and again, and my hands drifted down over her curves as I pinned her up against the wall. Her lips yielded almost instantly to mine. Her body arched forward against me.

She was breathless, and I did not let her breathe. I wanted to cover her with my kisses.

I shoved her hips back, pinning them tightly against the wall. She yelped as my mouth moved down to her neck, sucking hard under the collar. Not hard enough to leave any marks. Just enough for a taste. She was sweet and salty and I licked her neck, wanting more.

"_Ohh_—" she cried.

I kissed her again, sucking the breath from her lungs. My hand slid down under her panties, and I was shocked to find her already soaking wet. Even though I'd just come, I was instantly hard again.

"Fuck, Jessica. Look at how wet you are."

My fingers slid along her dripping slit. I stroked lightly, teasing little strokes. She squirmed against me, soft cries escaping her lips as I stroked her under her panties. My fingers dipped into that sweetness, and I could feel her clenching against me.

"I want you. Jessica, oh God, Jessica."

I wanted to taste her so badly. I wanted to give her the same pleasure she had just given me. My hands tore her panties down. She yelped as I shoved down the fabric and grabbed at my hands.

"Vale," she said.

It was the sound of my name on her lips. She'd never said my name like that before. It made me pause. In an instant, I blinked and saw her as she really was. Her wrists were cuffed, the chains running outward on both sides. She had a collar around her throat. I had her trapped. She was a prisoner.

She was *my* prisoner.

I tensed up, pulling my hands away from her. Something in her face changed, as she looked up at me. A question in her face. This was all part of training for her, I realized. My stomach lurched.

My prisoner.

"Vale?"

I looked down into her innocent face, her hair haloed by the sunlight. Such a beautiful woman. She didn't deserve this. Not at my hand, not at anyone's hand. I hated myself then for what I had done to her. Dirty work? This was way past dirty. This was wrong.

"I'm sorry," I said quietly. "I'll stop now. You did so well. You're perfect. I don't... I'm sorry."

I bit my lip, unable to form another sentence. Her eyes searched my face. I don't know what she was looking for, but whatever it was, she wouldn't find it. I was blank, empty. I was hollow with the horror of what I'd done. She didn't look scared anymore, though. As she looked into my eyes, I saw a deep well of courage inside of her.

More than that, though, I could see that some small part of her was suffused with desire. It was there, clear as day, and despite everything, I found myself hoping that her desire was real.

Then her lips parted. Her voice trembled, but when she spoke, it was an order, not a question.

"Vale. Don't stop."

Chapter Twenty-Six

Jessica

I couldn't stand the thought of him leaving me again, unsatisfied and longing for release.

That wasn't the reason I told him not to stop, though. It was the reason I told myself. But a darker part of me knew the truth: I loved the way he touched me.

I loved the way he pressed my hips back into the wall with his strong hands. I loved that he tore kisses from my mouth, ripping my breath away. And a terrible part of me loved that I was tied, that I couldn't do anything. He was completely in control of me, no matter how I controlled his desire.

He's the bad guy.

My mind reminded me over and over again, but it didn't matter. My body responded to his touch with absolutely no concern for dignity or morality. There was no right or wrong, my body told me. There was only the thick burning feeling that made me ache for him to touch me, to kiss me.

Would he fuck me now?

I'd told him not to stop, but I realized as I did that I had no idea what he was going to do with me. And just as quickly, my body told me that I wanted whatever he had to offer. His cock in my mouth had turned on the fire inside my core. When he'd shoved his hand down my panties, I knew what he wanted. I wanted it too, at least part of me did.

Vale went back to the door, tightened the chains on the wall, all the while looking at me. My arms went tight, the chains pulling them out on both sides of my body. He came back over, still staring at me with a strange look on his face. A gentle look.

He's the bad guy.

He bent his head and kissed me. I lifted my chin, parting my lips, but the kiss was just a brush of his lips. Then his hand wrapped around my throat just under the collar, and he tilted my chin to the side. His mouth fluttered soft kisses along my neck around the line of leather, down to my collarbone. Such delicate kisses, completely unlike the ones he'd given me before. The coil inside me wound tighter, and I clenched as he let his tongue slip out, darting small licks as he sank down. His hand slid under my bra, cupping my breast. Instead of kneading it, he brushed his thumb over the nipple. A shiver rippled through me.

"Ohh—" I started to cry, but he was already pulling my legs apart. No. He wasn't. He couldn't be.

"I want to taste you," he murmured. His voice was hoarse. It made me weak inside.

"Vale..."

He was kneeling now, and the coil inside me was tightening, tightening. All of my desire had been pent up, and now there was nothing to keep it back. When his tongue slid around my swollen clit, I cried out. A white starburst went off behind my eyes.

"Ohhhh!"

It was an orgasm unlike I'd ever given myself. The coil sprung with fiery speed. Explosive pleasure shuddered my body, and I felt my legs give way.

YOURS

If his hands hadn't been pinning my hips back against the wall, I would have slid to the floor. Every part of my body was liquid, it seemed. Nothing was real anymore, everything shook and trembled.

His tongue swirled around me, sending ripple after ripple of energy shivering through me. The waves of orgasm ripped through me again and again, burning through my body like wildfire.

I realized that I was whimpering, squirming slowly above him.

"That was fast," he said. I could tell without looking that he was smiling.

Then his hands lifted from my hips. I braced myself against the wall. The stone was cool under my fingers. It was the only cool thing in the room. The air had turned sweltering.

Instead of standing, though, he slipped both of his hands between my legs. Before I could realize what he was doing, he had hooked my knees over his arms and was holding me up. His face was planted firmly between my thighs.

"Vale!"

"Yes?"

He glanced up. I had a sudden urge to brush my fingers through the short tousled hair. What was happening to me? But my hands couldn't reach his hair, not with the chains on. I was helpless as he bent his head again, his breath coming hot against my throbbing clit.

"What are you doing?"

"Making you come again. What does it look like I'm doing?"

"Wh—why?" There was no reason for this. It was all

manipulation, wasn't it? The smile on his face looked so damn real.

"You deserve it, darling. You're such a good girl."

Vale dipped his tongue down, pushing against the spot where the throbs of my orgasm were already waning.

"Vale—oh! Vale!"

I couldn't stop it, not even if I had wanted to. And I didn't want to. For all of my life, I'd tried to be a good girl. I'd done whatever was asked of me, no matter how difficult. I'd sacrificed my own feelings for everyone around me. I'd worked hard, and for what? For my future. Always, always, looking ahead to the future.

Now, with no future ahead of me, I could do what I wanted to do in the present.

And this—this terrible, dark passion—this was what I wanted.

"Jessica, darling."

He was bad, and I was bad for wanting him, but we were already in Hell and there was no place worse for sinners to be sent to. So I sinned. I opened myself up to the pleasures he was offering. And I enjoyed every dark moment of it.

"Vale," I moaned.

Now his hand reached down, meeting the place where his mouth was already on me. His fingers slid over my slit, where I was already dripping wet. They curled, and I felt his knuckles probe me.

I could see my shadow on the floor, both of our shadows together, dark on the stone. The sun coming in from behind me was hot on my back, but not nearly as hot as the burning inside of me. I ached for more, more, and I let my shame spiral away as I fell into my own desire.

He stretched me, his fingers slowly thrusting deeper and deeper. His thick strong hands worked my clit even as he sucked me there, his lips sealing around my swollen nub.

I jerked my head from side to side, my nerves firing more and more as his tongue flicked me.

"Oh! Ohhh!"

Then his thumb was in my opening and he was stroking all around my entrance, the delicious friction between the pads of his fingers and my slickness.

"OHHHH!"

It hadn't been more than a few minutes, but already I was at the edge. Our shadows had merged and there was only one shadow, and I fell forward, my arms taut against the chains. My hips rocked into his mouth and he thrust his knuckles up into me.

I couldn't help it. I needed him. Needed his mouth, his lips, his tongue. I needed his fingers, curled and thick inside me. I needed him to stretch me even more. He met my rocking rhythm and matched it, and whatever rational thoughts I might have had went flying out the window with the unbearable sensation.

"*OHHHH!*"

He sent me soaring over the edge into yet another orgasm. This one unraveled me completely, and I jerked against the chains, bucking wildly into the seal of his lips. He sucked hard, flicking me with his tongue, and I wrenched from side to side as the dark climax spread through me and covered me completely.

"Yes," I whispered. I was undone. I would do anything he wanted. I would obey him. "Yes."

The door lock behind us rattled.

"Vale!"

There was a knock on the door, three sharp raps. Vale stood up quickly, catching me in his arms as my legs went limp. I scrambled to regain my balance, pushing away from his strong chest and leaning against the wall instead. Dizziness flooded my brain.

"What is it?"

Vale was already clambering into his clothes, swiping a hand through his short hair. The voice boomed through the door.

"El Alfa wishes to see you."

"I'll be there in a—"

"Right now."

Vale swore. He buttoned the last part of his shirt and turned back to me.

"Thank you," he said. Bending down, he kissed me fiercely, once, then turned away. He quickly did up the chains, then opened the iron door. El Alfa's head henchman was standing there, an ugly grimace on his face.

"I'm coming," Vale snapped. The door slammed behind him as they moved off down the hallway. Soon their voices disappeared.

I slumped down against the wall. Every part of me felt delicate, like crystal. I wrapped my arms around myself to keep from shattering.

He had unwound me completely. He had shown me a part of myself I never knew existed. I hadn't known what passion was before today, not truly. I'd let myself go, and I'd fallen hard and fast for him.

He's the bad guy.

The chain on my left hand rattled, and I tugged on it. But rather than feel the taut restraint, as I had already gotten used to, there was no resistance. I tugged again. The chain slid through the hook, clinking quickly in a metallic slithering motion, until the end came to rest on top of the heap of chain.

I blinked hard. For a second, my mind was too fuzzy to even realize what had happened. And then I blinked again, and it was clear.

He had forgotten to lock the chain.

I could escape.

Chapter Twenty-Seven

Vale

I stepped into El Alfa's room not knowing what to expect. What I saw, however, struck ice cold terror into my heart.

In front of me, past a low table, there was a woman attached to a large chain that hung from the ceiling in the middle of the room. Rope ran around her arms, her waist, her legs. The knots forced apart her thighs. Her back was bloody. There was desperation in her eyes.

El Alfa stood in front of the woman, facing away from me, a whip in his hand. Had he seen me yet? I doubted it.

In an instant, I took in the rest of my surroundings. The walls were covered in huge paintings and tapestries. As I turned my eyes away from the woman, unable to bear to look at her, I saw that they, too, showed acts of terror. Paintings of war, scenes of torture, hung on every wall. There was no getting away from it.

I stepped forward to the table that separated us. It was covered in what looked like torture instruments. Ropes, whips, straps. Handcuffs. Gags.

I fingered the handle of a red whip. It was a cat o'nine tails. The red leather was carved ornately at the top, and then the whip split apart. Each smooth tapered leather strap dripped with blood.

My heart pounded. I grabbed the leather whip in my hand. It was almost time to kill him; too early, but I might not get a better option. I could choke him to death, the bastard. I was around the table, two steps away from him, when he turned around.

"Vale?"

I stopped, looking down. He had a gun in his waistband, and his hand brandished the whip menacingly. I could probably take him—probably, but I wasn't sure whether to risk it.

"You called for me?" I asked.

El Alfa squinted at me as he came forward. The waft of his breath hit my nose with a palpable wave of smell— he was stinking drunk.

"What is this?" he asked, gesturing at the red leather I held with a faint smile. "Why do you have a whip, Americano?"

I could have jumped him. I didn't know how fast he could pull the gun from its holster. But no. It was still a few days before the raid. I couldn't kill him yet.

The decision made, I had to deflect his suspicion. I smiled as though amused by the scene of torture in front of me.

"I thought you called me here to join in," I said, waggling the leather strap in my hand. "No?"

The woman whimpered. El Alfa roared with laughter.

A small burst of relief made my grip relax. Good. Then he didn't suspect me.

"Go," he said, gesturing to a small bar on the side of the room. "Pour yourself a drink. Pour me one, too."

Walking over, I eyed the girl and tried to assess her wounds. It didn't look like she was in any sort of imminent danger. There were a lot of wounds, the blood trickling down from dozens of places, but none of the cuts were deep. She wasn't going to die.

I picked up the tequila and raised an eyebrow, waving it in the air.

"This okay?"

"Yes," El Alfa said, nodding with approval. His fat fingers stroked the whip. When I brought over his glass, he switched the whip to his other hand. Dare I make a move now? No. I had to wait. The raid would be here soon, and I was doing my job making sure that he trusted me. I was following orders. I sipped the tequila and kept my cool. The taste of it was bitter in my mouth.

El Alfa slammed back the tequila I'd poured—more than two shots worth. He smacked his lips and grinned at me. I could see drops of the tequila shining on the ends of his black, black mustache.

"You have done a good job," he slurred. "Your girl is obeying, yes?"

"Yes," I said cautiously.

"This one, not so much."

He raised the whip and brought it down sharply against the woman's side. She screamed. Although the sound went scraping across my nerves, I tried not to seem bothered by it.

"What happened with this one?" I asked. El Alfa clearly wanted to tell me. Maybe this was another lesson for me, his new protégé.

"This one, she tried to escape," he said, whipping her again. "A bad example for the others."

"How did she escape?"

"How? There is only one way to escape. Through my room here."

He laughed at nothing. I started laughing along with

him. I wanted him drunk, in a good mood. I wanted him to show me everything. I wanted him to trust me.

"This room?" I said, letting a tone of disbelief enter my words.

"It is true!" He laughed and laughed, and I laughed along. His cheeks were turning red.

"No!" I said. My astonishment wasn't hard to feign. "You have a secret escape here?"

"Yes."

"Impossible. I don't believe it. How did she really escape?"

"Ho! Americano! Come look."

He was drunk enough to show me. He came over to the bar. Instead of pouring a drink, though, he reached under the bar and pressed something that made a slight "click" sound.

I stared agape at him as he handed me the secret I'd been waiting for.

One of his hanging rugs rolled up to reveal a metal door. There was a keypad inset in the door itself.

A secret door. It made sense, but I didn't understand how Ten had gone through two raids without figuring out where the exit was.

El Alfa pressed his thumb against the keypad, and the metal door slid open. Behind the door was a dimly lit set of stone stairs that led down steeply into darkness.

"This is how she got out?" I let my genuine amazement show. This was a smart set up. A personalized thumbpad lock to make sure nobody could use the door without El Alfa being there himself. The door itself hidden by an automated cover. The switch to the cover hidden inside the bar.

I would have thought El Alfa was a brilliant man, except that he had the same character flaw I did: pride. He wanted to show off his pretty things. His women, his secrets. It was nothing if he couldn't brag about them to someone else.

And now that someone else was me.

El Alfa was still talking excitedly and gesturing with the hand that held the whip.

"The last time the police try to get me, whew! It was quick. A close call. I couldn't leave her in my room. We both went down."

"Wow! Does it go right out to the street?" I asked, making my question casual. I didn't want him to figure out that I was prying for information. But he was so drunk that I didn't think he would have noticed if I flashed an FBI badge in his face. This was his personal mansion, and he was showing it off to his new best friend. If I hadn't been so disgusted with him, I might have pitied him.

"To the beach. Then to a boat. Only she managed there to get away from me."

"How?"

"She jumped—bam!— into the ocean! I thought she was dead. It was a very big storm, and I could not find her anywhere in the water."

"Bad luck. About the weather, I mean," I said sympathetically.

"Yes, yes. But after the raid was over, my men managed to track her down," El Alfa said. There was a sick gleam in his eye.

"And now?"

"Now?"

"You said you didn't want to… uh, damage the girls,"

I said.

"Well, she is no use to me anymore. A runaway? Bah. No good to sell. But as an example to the others…"

"I see."

"Yes, you see. You are doing very well with the training," El Alfa said.

"Thank you," I said. "I'm looking forward to doing more."

"More?"

"With the girl you have me training, I mean." I hated to mention Jessica, but he had brought up the training. The next thing he said, though, made me freeze.

"Oh. Oh, that is too bad. They will be leaving this weekend."

I swallowed hard, taking in his meaning before I spoke again.

"This—this weekend?"

"Si. Antigua wants them earlier than usual. We'll ship them out on Saturday."

I nodded absently, as though I didn't care overmuch. But inside, my heart was pounding. I wanted to grab him by the shirt and press him for more details, but I had to take what I could get.

Saturday. That was the day before the raid. It would be harder to get El Alfa alone just before then, if he was preparing to move the girls.

And he was shipping them out. To Antigua? I couldn't let him do that. If Jessica was shipped out—

What was I thinking? The mission wasn't about Jessica. It wasn't about the girls. The mission was clear: kill El Alfa right before the raid. I had my orders. I had to follow them.

I refocused my attention on El Alfa, who was still talking.

"You will help with the transport. I think if you do well with the training, you can have your own house and handle all the training. You like that, yes?"

I smiled. It was the coldest smile I had ever managed to put on. My whole body felt numb, unfeeling.

"Will I be able to keep the girl?" I didn't know how I was going to manage to keep El Alfa from sending all the girls away to another country. But I knew one thing—I had to figure out a way to get this done soon, or else the raid would turn up empty... again. And Jessica would be lost to me.

"Keep her? For good?"

"Just for a bit longer," I said, trying desperately to appear casual. "I'm not done training her yet."

"Of course," El Alfa said, smiling so broadly I could see the gold glint of fillings in his back teeth. "She is yours."

Mine. I had to do something in the next couple of days to save her. Or we would both be lost.

Chapter Twenty-Eight

Jessica

I was still throbbing with warmth from the orgasms Vale had given me, but now adrenaline pumped through my system. Escape was only a few feet away!

I pulled the chain all the way through its loops. I was still chained on one side, but now I had slack.

One degree of freedom. It was all I needed.

The first thing I did was rip off the collar that was around my neck. It was easy enough to unclip the hasp. I tossed the collar into the corner. Gone. I wasn't going to be a slave anymore.

I stumbled over to the wall, still in disbelief, pulling one of the chains behind me. I stared at the metal door that Vale had left through. Was it locked? I could only hope not. I tried to be as quiet as I could as I moved forward toward the door.

The remaining chain caught me before I could make it there. I stretched out, but couldn't reach the place where the chain was locked by the door. It threaded through an iron loop in the wall, and that's where I was leashed. Just out of reach, like a dog chained to a stake.

No. I wasn't going to let that stop me. My mind worked quickly to see what I needed to do to get out of here.

If I could get the metal loop to give, I would be able to reach the door and unlock the last chain. My fingers traveled over the iron bolts. They were rusty. Hopefully rusty enough to break.

As I began to pry the loop from where it was bolted into the wall, I paused. Was this a test? Was it a game? What if Vale was standing right outside the room in the hallway, waiting for me to escape? What if all of this was a trap?

I'd have to take that chance.

As quietly as I could, I grabbed hold onto the chain on either side of the bolt. I felt weak. I wished I had eaten more when Vale had offered me food. Now, my arms felt like hell as I used all my muscles to strain against the iron loop.

It moved. Just a bit, a tiny shift, but it moved. I could do it. With the right leverage, I could do it. I wrapped the chain around my hands on both sides and pushed my foot against the wall. The stone felt cold and rough under my bare foot, but I could feel the iron bolt giving way as I tugged.

Once, twice. I heard a noise and looked over at the metal door. No, it wasn't anything. I was hearing things. I looked back over to the other side of the room, where the window was. The sunlight was blinding. I'd been used to having it at my back, but now that I stared at the back wall, everything looked brighter.

Again! I tugged hard and heard a creak as the rusted iron bolt strained under my pressure. Then again!

The bolt snapped in two, and I managed to pull the loop out of the wall with one final jerk of the chain. It ripped the bolt from the wall and clattered to the ground. I waited for a second, sure that the noise would have alerted the guards. There were footsteps outside of my room. I grabbed the chains that were still attached to my wrists.

They were the only weapons I had at my disposal.

Then the footsteps stopped. So did my breath. The guard outside waited for a second more and then left, his steps disappearing down the hall outside the door. I let out a relieved sigh.

Two degrees of freedom.

I was at the hook by the door. It was easy enough to uncoil the chain from around the hook. Then I pulled it through the loops and looked down.

Two long chains. And they were still attached to my wrists by the black leather cuffs. I tried to pick one up and sling it over my shoulder. It was heavy, each iron link clinking and pinching at my skin. I dropped the chain back down, panting. I couldn't very well go and try to escape with a hundred pounds of iron tied to each wrist.

Okay, well, I couldn't escape like this. How could I get out of these chains? I'd thought that the hardest part would be getting the chains unlocked, but now that I'd done that, I was still stuck.

I couldn't freak out. I took another deep breath in, then out. I could do this. I wasn't going to let Vale come back and find me here. I was going to escape.

I examined the cuffs. I hadn't been able to see them closely when my arms had been stretched apart, but now I could turn them around to get a look. There was a metal lock on the inside of the cuffs that they had used to lock them on. What could I use to undo the locks?

There was nothing inside this cell that was small enough to pick a lock. Oh, if only I had kept the breakfast plate Vale had given me! A fork might have been small enough to jam inside the lock. But even if I did that, I didn't have any idea of how to unlock the thing.

This wasn't going to work. I was too much of a good girl. I'd never picked a lock… I'd never even thought about picking a lock. I was useless here. Desperation bubbled up inside of me. I slumped back against the wall under the window where I'd originally been tied up.

Then I looked at the backs of the cuffs. I lifted them into the square of sunlight. They were tied up with knotted leather lace.

Maybe I couldn't undo the lock, but a few knots? I could do this. I think I could do this.

I started work on the first cuff. It was slow going—it took me almost fifteen minutes to undo the first knot. But now that I knew how to do it, I knew that it was possible. It might take forever, but it was possible.

It would have been much, much easier if I could have worked with both hands, but the knots were on the back of the cuff where I couldn't reach with my fingers. So I worked one-handed.

It was afternoon already. By the time I had the cuffs off, it would be night time. I would have to hope that nobody would come down to my cell. Not Vale, not El Alfa, not any of the guards. Sure, it was a dim glimmer of hope, but it was all I had to work with.

Patiently, one piece at a time, I began to unravel the tightly knotted cuff.

Chapter Twenty-Nine

Vale

The sun was setting outside the huge window. The last red rays of the sun reflected off of the crashing waves just outside El Alfa's estate. I sipped on my tequila, waiting for my orders.

El Alfa finally slumped back on the couch in exhaustion. He pushed a button on the end table.

Immediately two girls in white gauze dresses came in. They didn't look at the bed, where the other girl was still hanging from her chains. They went straight to him and knelt in front of him. Their hands lay out in front of them, palms up.

"Help me to the baths," El Alfa said. The girls rose and took his fat, meaty hands, pulling him to his feet. He lurched away, leaning hard to one side.

I could follow them. I could kill him now. But orders were orders, and I was supposed to wait until just before the raid. I met El Alfa's eye, and he noticed me standing there as though for the first time.

"Do what you want with her," El Alfa slurred, gesturing to the girl who had tried to run away. "Have fun, Americano."

He left, the two girls supporting his weight. The door slammed shut behind him.

My eyes fell on the girl hanging over the bed. She was still bleeding from her wounds. A dirty gag was stuffed in her mouth. I stepped closer and picked up a knife from the table full of torture instruments. I could use it later, maybe. Of all the tools here, El Alfa wouldn't miss one. It was a small knife, the blade thin and sharp. Bile rose in my throat as I thought about what El Alfa might have used it for.

If El Alfa asked, I would say that I wanted to use it as a threat for Jessica during her training. He would believe me, I thought. He trusted me, at least enough to let me into his private rooms. I could only hope that he would trust me further.

That he would trust me until he was dead.

I stepped forward and the girl moaned in terror behind her gag.

She thought I was going to hurt her. Of course.

I tucked the knife back in my belt on the side. I adjusted my shirt so that the folds nearly covered the handle. It wouldn't be apparent to anyone unless they were paying close attention.

The girl wriggled on the chain, like bait hung in the ocean to catch fish. I was the shark, or so she thought. But I wasn't here to eat her. No, far from it. I couldn't help her much, but I could get her away from El Alfa, at least. He'd said I could do what I liked with her. So I would keep him to that promise.

I pulled the gag from her mouth. She didn't meet my eyes as I tossed the gag aside. Her attention was at my belt, at the place where I'd put the knife.

"It's alright," I said, without much conviction. It wasn't alright, not for her. But at least she didn't have to fear me. When I reached out for her, she flinched away.

"I won't hurt you," I said.

How many times had I said that since coming here? Ten's orders had been simple: do whatever I had to do in order to get at El Alfa. Here I was, trying to justify acting the way I did. But I had hurt Jessica—I'd hurt her, badly. I'd scared her to death. I'd killed her friend. And now I was making promises to another girl, promises that I couldn't keep if El Alfa ordered me otherwise.

I untied her hands. She slumped down, and I picked her up, feeling her light weight in my arms. Like a ghost of a person. She was bruised on all sides, and she whimpered as I carried her out of El Alfa's rooms, but she didn't scream again.

I brought her down the stairs. There was a cell near Jessica's that I knew was empty. I could put her there.

From out of the shadows, a figure appeared.

"What do you have there?"

It was David. That asshole.

"A girl." I spoke abruptly, as though he was interrupting something important. But he only came forward and leaned on the wall, leering at the girl's cuts. There was an evil gleam in his face as his eyes dragged down over her bruised body.

"What happened?"

"She tried to run away."

"You did this to her?"

There was a clinking sound, and I looked down the hallway. Nothing. All of the doors were shut. I frowned. It had sounded like —but never mind. I had to deal with David now.

I kicked open the door, since David didn't seem to want to open the door for me. He walked in behind us.

"El Alfa and I both had our fun," I explained. I hoped that would be enough to satisfy him.

As I set the girl down, I heard the sound of his belt

unbuckling.

"Then I'll have mine, too."

I glared back at him.

"She's had enough."

"Says who?"

"Says me. She's no good to El Alfa if she's dead."

He scowled at me.

"You're nobody here. Understand? If I told El Alfa—
"

"Go tell him then."

I stood there, staring implacably. I dared him silently to go upstairs, where El Alfa was in all likelihood asleep in a bathtub, being washed by the two girls in white gauze dresses.

I shouldn't have been pressing my luck. All I had to do was hold out for two more days, and then I could kill the man. But the thought of David doing anything with this poor, broken girl made me feel ill.

She whimpered behind me. I clicked the armcuffs around her wrists, going through the motions of chaining her up. I ignored David as best as I could, working slowly and methodically. Eventually, he got tired of waiting.

David slammed the door as he left. I could hear his footsteps clanging down the hallway and up the stairs.

I stayed for a few minutes, washing the girl's wounds as best as I could with a dirty linen cloth I found on the floor. As I'd expected, most of the cuts were superficial, and the deeper bruises were beyond my help. She needed rest, that was all.

Rest. That's what I needed too, after all this. I thought of going next door, to Jessica. I wanted to take her in my arms and tell her everything.

Stupid, I know. What was I thinking? I wanted comfort. How selfish was I, that I would think of trying to take comfort in the arms of a girl who was, for all intents and purposes, my prisoner?

I heard a clink from out in the hallway. My ears perked up.

I pushed the door open and stepped out quickly. To my astonishment, Jessica was standing there in the hallway, completely unchained. Her face froze in terror.

"Jessica—" I said, holding my hand out.

She turned and ran.

Chapter Thirty

Jessica

Vale stood right in front of me. I heard his words from before, tolling a warning bell in my head.

A girl—

She tried—

She tried to run away.

My worst nightmare had come true. He was only an arm's length away. He looked as shocked as I did that I wasn't tied up. Well, I wasn't going to give him any time to figure it out.

"Jessica—"

I spun and darted away, down the hallway. I didn't know where I was going, only that I couldn't let him catch me. I'd seen what happened to girls who tried to escape.

"Wait!"

His voice bounced off the end of the hallway, echoing back to me.

As I reached the stairs, his hand gripped my arm. I kicked backwards as hard as I could. I must have hit him squarely in the stomach, because he grunted and his hand loosened. I ripped away from him and scrambled up the stairs.

"Jessica—stop—"

He caught my foot and I fell down, knocking my head against the wall. The torch light spun dizzily in my vision. I heard footsteps coming from above.

"No!" I cried out.

Vale dragged me back and slung me over his shoulder. I beat at his back with my fists, but it was like beating on the surface of water—useless. Still, I hit him, let all of my fear and frustration out through the blows against his impenetrable exterior.

"Stop it," he growled. He ducked down to carry me through the cell door. My fingers slid uselessly over the metal door, scrabbling against the stone entryway for only a split second before he had pulled me back inside. The iron door clanged shut behind us, and I let out a cry of disbelief. I had been so close—so close—

"Stop it!"

I realized that I was moaning, stretching my hands toward the locked door. Vale set me down on the floor as I twisted. Then I saw it.

The handle of a knife sticking out from behind his belt.

I reached out and pulled it without thinking. The knife turned, and I saw the blood seeping red against Vale's shirt before I heard him swear.

"Fuck!"

I leapt backward and Vale took a step back, too. We faced off, only a few feet apart. I crouched under the window in the back of the cell. My foot braced back against the wall. If he came close, then, at least I would have leverage. The light from the window might have blinded him, if only it had been earlier in the day. Now it was almost night time, and the light was dim. All of my luck was bad luck, but I was desperate. I had to take any chance I could get.

He shifted toward me and I raised the knife. My hand trembled. The blade glinted in the reddish rays from the window, sending dim sprays of reflected light across the ceiling of the cell.

"Jessica, stop. You don't know how to fight with a knife."

"The easiest way is to slit the throat," I said, parroting him. "Or through the ribs. I should be holding the blade sideways, right?"

"Jessica—"

He moved slightly forward and I jabbed the knife in the air. He stopped, his hands raised to protect himself. His face was solemn, but I could still see his muscles tensed. Ready to catch me.

"Or the femoral artery."

"I'm not here to hurt you," he said.

"Really? You're not here to hurt me? That's pretty fucking unbelievable, considering what you did to that other girl."

His face paled slightly. He turned to glance at the door, shifting his weight as he did. I shifted mine. I wasn't going to let him take me off-guard. He turned back to me.

"You saw that?"

"I was going to escape then, but I saw you and that guy outside and closed the door. I saw her, too. Don't tell me—"

"El Alfa did that to her."

"Sure," I hissed. "*El Alfa* did that to her. And *El Alfa* made you kill James. And *El Alfa* made you fuck me—"

"I am not going to hurt you," Vale said, a frown drawing together on his brow.

"That's damn right you're not going to hurt me. Or I'll stab you. Now get out of my way."

He stepped sideways then, lunging at my arm. I sliced

the knife across the air, but it only nicked his arm. He was already stepping back between me and the door. Blood dripped from the shallow cut on his arm.

"Stay. Back."

"I can't let you out that door, Jessica."

"Why?"

"You know why. They'll hurt you. El Alfa will hurt you."

"I'll take my chances." He was bleeding from his arm and his side, and still he didn't want to get out of my way.

"You don't understand."

"No? Then explain."

A cloud moved over his face. I realized that the sun had gone away dipped below the horizon, and the cell was dimmer. He shook his head.

"I can't."

"Then get out of my way."

"Don't make me do this, Jessica." He took one step toward me. I held up the knife. I'd already gotten him twice. I could do it. I could stab him.

As he moved forward, his arm came up to grab me on the right. I sliced the knife in that direction, but he was already out of the way, spinning left. He moved faster than I'd ever seen anyone move before. In an instant, he had gripped my arm.

"No!"

I twisted to try and get away, but his other arm came around me. He spun back against the wall, holding my body tightly against his. I kicked, but he picked me up off of my feet. My wrist was held as though by pincers in his rough, strong fingers.

"Stop! Let me go!"

I squirmed, but he only squeezed my wrist harder. A shock of pain stabbed through my arm. I yelped, my fingers loosening. The knife clattered to the stone floor.

"No! *NO!*"

My only weapon. My only hope. Gone.

He kicked the knife away with his shoe. It spun off into the dark corner of the cell. I felt my muscles weaken. The shot of adrenaline through my body had worn its course, and it hadn't been enough.

Now my heart beat fast with terror. I was going to die, or worse. I'd seen a glimpse of what they'd done to the girl in the cell next to me. The one who'd tried to run away. She had been covered in blood. I let out a cry of defeat as Vale spun me around.

"Jessica."

I closed my eyes, waiting for the first blow. My breath came fast and I could hear the rush of blood in my ears. A second passed, then another. I felt his hand cup my cheek, and I trembled.

"Please—"

"Jessica, look at me."

My eyelids fluttered open. I saw Vale's icy blue eyes.

"Don't hurt me. Please—please don't do to me what you did to her. Oh, God."

"I told you. I'm not going to hurt you."

He backed away from me slowly and picked up the knife. He tucked it back into his belt, this time on the other side. I stood shakily as he held up one of the leather cuffs. The knots were all undone. Was that a smile on his lips? It couldn't be.

He tossed the useless cuff back down.

"Wait here," he said.

Before I could respond, the iron door was closing behind him. I waited for only a second before darting forward. The image of that girl in his arms, her hair red with blood—I couldn't wait here. But he was too quick, and as my hand touched the iron door handle, it swung back open. I lunged to get past him, but he shoved me back into the cell easily. I scrambled back as he moved toward me.

"I told you to wait here."

"Please, no," I said. There was another leather collar in his hand, this one with a thicker silver clasp. "Don't. Please don't put it on me—"

"You can't leave this room."

"Please."

"Kneel."

I gritted my teeth, but there was no way to escape. I had to do what he said.

I fell to my knees, tears streaming down my cheeks. I had tried to escape. Tried and failed. My hands came out in front of me. Palms up. My tears dripped onto the stone floor as I bent my head forward.

The collar came around my neck. The chain rattled as he attached it, his strong hand brushing my shoulder. The lock clicked shut.

I was on a leash now.

Sobs choked my throat. It was over. I would never escape. I would never save April. I was locked up for good this time.

"Jessica—"

"Kill me."

The words escaped my mouth before I could stop them. I felt his hesitation, his hand on my shoulders as he knelt down in front of me. Was he pulling his knife out with his other hand? I hoped so.

"Kill me," I repeated numbly. "Please. Just kill me."

"Jessica—"

"I don't want to be here forever," I said. I looked up into his eyes. "Please."

He blinked, his dark lashes flickering over glassy blue irises. Then the veil lifted, and his face filled with concern.

"Oh, Jessica."

Before I could say anything, he was kissing me, a slow soft kiss that shocked me so badly I didn't move. His hands cupped my face, brushing away my tears as he deepened the kiss. Heat shot through me and my lips parted, opening myself up to him.

Resist him? It was impossible. I let out a cry as my own body responded traitorously to his lips pressing against mine.

Then, just as suddenly, he tore away from me. My eyes refocused onto his face, his expression tense. Was he afraid?

"Don't leave this room," he said. "Not yet. It's too dangerous."

"Vale?"

"*Trust me.*"

There was a secret in his face, something that I couldn't read yet. But it was there, I knew it. Something beyond his icy exterior. Something even more dangerous than before. He looked like a completely different person.

"Who are you?"

I could hear footsteps coming down the hallway. Vale swiveled his head to look. The tendons in his neck were taut, standing out under his skin.

"I can't tell you now. Trust me. *You will not be in here forever.* I promise."

"But—"

The door opened.

Chapter Thirty-One

Vale

"El Alfa."

I stood up, straightening myself. The knife was still in my hand, and I pretended to tuck my shirt back in, pocketing the knife into my belt as I did so.

"I wanted to see how your training was coming along," he asked. His words were slurred, and his hair was wet. I wondered if he'd had another drink after his bath.

"It's fine."

I had one more day. One more day to pretend, and then I could kill him. There were two guards in the hallway now. Killing him down here wouldn't be ideal, and I dismissed the idea.

"Excellent. I'm glad to hear it."

"We were just finishing—"

"I would like to see a demonstration."

I stiffened. Behind me, Jessica cowered.

"Of course."

I gestured for El Alfa to come into the cell. As he did, his eyes traced down my shirt to where Jessica had sliced through me with a knife. The shirt was stained red with blood. Even though he was drunk, his attention narrowed onto the cut.

"You have cut yourself?"

"It's nothing." I waved it off. "An accident with a knife."

He tilted his head toward Jessica.

"Did you cut the girl?"

"No."

"Then why take the knife?"

Shit. He had seen it. I tried not to act out of the ordinary.

"Only as a threat," I said lightly. "I wanted to make it clear to her that disobedience would be punished."

"We don't allow knives down here," he said. "Or they might end up in the wrong hands."

He held out his hand. Slowly, I drew the knife from behind my belt and laid it in his palm. He looked at me. Was he suspicious?

"Now," he said. "Show me how you've trained her."

I turned around and licked my lip nervously. I could control my behavior. But Jessica? She was a wild card. I could only hope that she understood that she would have to perform for El Alfa. And that meant following my orders.

"Kneel," I commanded.

For a split second, when she met my eye, I thought she wouldn't listen to me. A flash of fear went through my chest. But she obeyed.

Falling to her feet, she put her arms out in front of her. Her wrists turned, palms up. I could see the marks from her wrists cuffs where she'd taken them off.

"Good work," El Alfa said. "Can she do more?"

"Of course," I said, hedging. "But we've been working for a while now—"

"Show me."

Jessica looked up with a burst of terror passing over her face. All of the time I'd spent trying to get her to trust me was useless now, unless she did what El Alfa

182

commanded.

I stepped in front of her so that El Alfa couldn't see. With a sympathetic expression, I mouthed the words: *Trust me.*

She nodded, a quick sharp motion meant to be hidden from El Alfa. And although we had stalled for a few moments, El Alfa seemed drunk enough that he didn't notice the pause.

"Sit up," I ordered.

She sat up, kneeling on the hard floor. I ached for her as she suffered, the suffering itself written in winces whenever she shifted her weight slightly. El Alfa moved over to the side of the wall where one chain hung loosely. It was the other one that was attached to her, at the collar.

I hoped that he didn't notice that the wrist cuffs had been unraveled at the seams. The cuffs lay off in one corner of the dim cell. It was then that I thanked whoever had kept light out of this place. In the shadows, the evidence of her escape attempt was invisible.

"Take off your bra," I ordered.

She obeyed me, and the bra fell to the floor. Not too far off from the cuffs.

"Cup them with your hands." She cradled her breasts in her palms. It was a performance, that was something I knew as well as she did. Still, though, my cock stiffened at the sight of her gorgeous breasts peeking out from behind her fingers.

I could tell she was unsure of what I was doing, but she did exactly what I said. A perfect submissive. El Alfa was right about that. He was wrong about a lot of other things, though. It was what I was counting on.

"Head back."

She leaned her head back, and I gripped her by the hair, pulling her back further in an apparent display of strength. I hoped El Alfa would notice only that I was pulling her hair, not that I was gripping it at the scalp where it hurt the least.

"Mmm." El Alfa scratched at his groin as he watched, obviously aroused. I was too, and I hoped that I wouldn't lose my arousal by going through these sadistic actions. As I looked down, though, Jessica licked her lips.

God, those lips. Those perfect, plump lips. I wanted to kiss them forever. As I watched, she chewed on one corner of her bottom lip. That was enough to make me hard for the rest of the night.

Alright, time to get this done with.

I unzipped my pants and took out my cock, already rock hard. She leaned forward, as though to take it in her mouth, but that wasn't what I intended. I jerked her head back by the hair. She gasped, a small gasp, as I took my cock in my hand and leaned down to her.

I spit on her chest. The splittle ran down between her breasts. She winced, but only a little.

El Alfa breathed in sharply. I didn't want to look over at him. I wasn't sure what he was doing over on the side of the cell, in the dim shadows. Maybe he was jerking it to us. Maybe. Who cared, as long as I could keep him distracted for another two days? That was all I needed... just two more days. Then I could kill him and stand by Jessica until the raid came to save us both.

"Stay still," I whispered, my eyes finding hers in the dim light. There was a trust in them that broke my heart. She trusted me, but only because she had to. Only because there was no other option.

Lifting Jessica up an inch farther, I thrust my cock between her breasts. She gasped. I breathed in too, hard. The delicious sensation of her smooth breasts taking my cock between them was almost too much.

Perfect breasts. Perfect lips. As I thrust in and out of that perfection, I could feel my orgasm pushing up hard and fast. Good. This would be over soon. I tilted her head up, my thumb accidentally grazing her lip.

She pressed a kiss onto the pad of my thumb. A shock of pleasure bolted through me. I gasped. My cock jumped up, coming out from the slick place between her breasts.

Before I could put it back in place, Jessica was moving. Her head bent down, and with one motion, she slid her mouth over the whole of my shaft. I cried out helplessly as she sealed her lips around my base, flicking her tongue at the bottom of my rock hard cock.

Again, I exploded in her mouth, falling forward to catch myself against the wall with one hand. My other hand still gripped her hair at the scalp.

She swallowed as the orgasm unspooled through my body, my hips pumping instinctively once more before I could gain control of my body again.

I panted, regaining my breath after the orgasm. God, it had been so quick. I was glad for that, for Jessica's sake. But she'd taken me again into her mouth, without me even giving the order…

This wasn't how I'd intended it to go, but El Alfa didn't know that.

El Alfa. I glanced over at the wall, where the drunken bastard was stroking the front of his pants with obvious arousal. His greasy black mustache twitched.

I wanted to kiss Jessica, to pull her up from the ground and cradle her in my arms. I wanted to give back to her what she had given to me, ten times over. But I couldn't. Not with him there.

Instead, I gave her an order.

"Kneel," I said hoarsely. Obedient, her eyes still questioning mine, she lay back down, her palms facing upward.

I turned around, stuffing myself back in my pants. I hated for El Alfa to see me like this, in this moment. It wasn't right. But right now, he was my boss, and I had to keep him happy.

For just a little longer. Two more days. And then I could kill him.

"Hope that was a good show," I said, tucking my shirt back into my belt. No knife. He'd taken my knife.

"You didn't fuck her," El Alfa said. A dark gleam shone from his beady black eyes. Like a rat. Rats never had enough. They took whatever they could, stole things that didn't belong to them, and they never, ever had enough.

"No," I agreed. I brushed past him, zipping my pants back up, and he grabbed my arm, clamping down with his meaty fingers on my sweaty skin.

"Why?"

I stopped in my tracks, my fingers absently doing up my pants. I wasn't sure what to tell him, what would be easiest. Finally, I settled on the truth.

"She's a virgin."

Now his eyes widened. Greed pulsed through his face as he licked his bottom lip, the pink tongue flicking out.

"A virgin?"

"I'm sure you'll get more money if she stays that

way," I said. "I thought—"

"You thought right. Good work, Americano."

He pushed by me and unclipped the chain from the wall. Slowly, drunkenly, he threaded it through the iron loops until it was no longer attached. Gathering it up in his hands, he tugged. Jessica rose by her collar, looking at me with blossoming fear in her eyes.

"What are you doing?" I asked.

"Taking her up to my room."

An icicle of fear dripped down my spine, chilling me all the way through.

"But—"

"You have done your job well, but a virgin is very...how do you say? *Valuable*. She will spend the night with me. Tomorrow they will all be shipped out."

My throat froze. I barely had time to comprehend what he was saying. I licked my lips and tried to speak calmly. Jessica's eyes sought mine, but I couldn't look at her. Not now. It would give me away if I had to look into her face.

"Tomorrow? But, that's only...I thought you said Saturday."

He looked at me as though I'd said something suspicious. I carefully made my expression neutral, realizing he'd lied to me before. He didn't trust me, not completely anyway.

"Tomorrow," he repeated flatly.

He was gone with her before I could process the thought, and the word echoed through my mind like a death sentence. Not my death sentence, but it might as well have been. The raid wasn't scheduled for another two days, but she was going to be gone.

Tomorrow.

Chapter Thirty-Two

Jessica

I was shaken by Vale, more shaken than I'd been by anything else since coming here. Even as El Alfa led me up a steep set of stairs by the collar, I couldn't help thinking about what Vale had said to me before it all had happened.

Trust me.

Was he only manipulating me, or was there something more? He hadn't said anything to El Alfa about my escape attempt. I wasn't sure if that was because Vale truly didn't want me to be hurt, or if he wanted me all to himself. And I wasn't sure what to make of the look between them when he'd told Vale that I was being shipped out somewhere tomorrow.

Shipped out? I didn't know if I was glad to be leaving, or if I was being sent to another place. Either way, I didn't want to leave without figuring out what was really going on with Vale.

God, I hated myself for how easy it had been for me to follow his orders. Even when El Alfa was standing there, watching, I couldn't stop my attention from focusing on Vale. His body was immense, hard and muscled. His very touch was possessive. When he'd told me to do something, I'd followed his orders instinctively.

Now, though, I didn't have him to instruct me.

Now, I was alone with El Alfa.

He yanked again on my collar. I stepped up the last step and out of the stairwell. I panted a little, catching my breath. It had been so many days since I'd last been able to move at all, and the act of climbing a steep stairwell was enough to make my heart pound.

A movement in the corner of my eye caught my attention. There was a woman sitting on a marble bench a little way down the hallway. Her dark hair fell in loose waves over her shoulders.

None of the other women I'd seen in the house had met my eyes, but she did. Her eyes were pools so dark that I could not tell where her irises stopped and her pupils began. And when she saw us, she stood.

With a feline swagger of the hips, she stalked over to us. Her lips plumped up as El Alfa noticed her, and she shook her dark hair back.

"Will you need me tonight, master?" she asked.

I couldn't believe her. Would anyone willingly go with El Alfa? I didn't think it was possible, but her hand was trailing down the sleeve of his shirt, her olive skin pristine and perfect. It was then that I realized she was the woman from the banquet, the one who had already been kneeling on the ground when I came in. She wasn't looking at me anymore, but at El Alfa.

"Not tonight, Valentina," he said. He patted her hand. "Maybe tomorrow."

She pouted, her lips plumping up even more. As though she was sad that she couldn't be the victim tonight. I cringed inside as El Alfa touched her.

Was this what I had become? After all, I'd followed Vale's commands. I was just as much a slave as she was. I was the one wearing the collar, after all. I didn't know if that was better or worse than having the illusion of freedom.

A tug on my collar took me out of my thoughts, and El Alfa pulled me across the marble floor toward what I imagined was his room.

I steeled myself for what I was going to face. I'd survived down in the cell, after all. I'd been able to make it through the training that Vale had given me. And though I imagined El Alfa's training would be much worse, I thought that I would be able to withstand it. I had to.

What I didn't realize was that I would have to withstand more than that.

El Alfa opened the door to his bedroom. He'd seemed very drunk downstairs, but now he was walking on steadier feet. He jerked the chain to my collar and led me into the room.

"*No*," I said, stopping in my tracks.

April was there. She was already chained up in the middle of the room. She was topless like me, a bruise running down her side. Her skin all along her waist was black and blue. There was a table—oh God, a table full of whips and knives. My heart sank.

"No," I said again. It was the only word that came to my lips.

No. No. No.

April was sobbing, and when she saw me it was like she didn't even recognize me. Her eyes were blank, empty pits of suffering.

The collar choked me as El Alfa yanked me forward. I hadn't realized that I had stopped in the middle of the doorway.

"Move, bitch," he muttered, pulling me forward. My feet walked as if of their own accord. I couldn't feel anything.

"You know her, don't you?" El Alfa asked. He hooked my chain up to the ceiling near April. Not near enough to touch her. I felt my hands ball into fists as I saw her bruise close up. The dark swelling looked too painful to breathe.

"Answer me!"

He slapped me across the cheek, and I realized that I hadn't said anything. I'd only been staring.

"Yes," I whispered. April looked back down, her hands clasped across her chest, already in cuffs. Tears streamed down her cheeks.

"You are perfect. A virgin princess, yes?"

I shuddered as his fingers trailed down my cheek. His black eyes were hungry. Greedy. He turned to April.

"But this one is not. A common whore, likely."

April sobbed. I wanted to take her into my arms and comfort her, but I was too far away. My whole body ached to act—to kill El Alfa, to hurt him, to escape. But the collar around my neck told me that I couldn't escape from here. I was trapped, waiting for my kidnapper to hurt me… or my best friend.

"You'll be worth a lot more on the selling block," El Alfa said, coming back to me. I stood as steady as I could while he put his hands on my hips, as though measuring me. His voice was a chilling whisper in my ear.

"Touch yourself."

I whipped my head around. El Alfa was smiling, a needle-thin smile. He was already unzipping his pants. I expected him to tell me to kneel.

But instead of me, he went to April.

"*No.*" The word died on my lips as he tore down her panties. Her sobs grew panicked, and I turned my head away.

"*Watch!*"

El Alfa's voice was a roar in the room. April's sobs grew fluttery and faint. I met El Alfa's eyes.

"Watch, and touch yourself," he said to me. "Do it or I'll whip her."

April screamed, a desperate scream, and he shoved a gag in her mouth. It was then that I realized why she didn't want to recognize me. She didn't want me to see her like this. This wasn't her.

"Do it!"

My hand moved down between my legs, but I was numb. All of my feelings went dim, and the tears blurred my eyes. I watched as he fucked her. I watched and cried, and couldn't do a damn thing.

When he was done, he sent her back down to the cells. Two guards came to take her away. She limped as she walked, and she didn't look at me again. I didn't look at her either. There wasn't anything I could do that would help.

I would kill him. I would kill them all for doing this.

Then she was gone, and El Alfa came back over to me. I thought he would send me back down too, but he didn't. As he walked toward me, he smiled, an awful, terrible smile that made the last of my tears dry up in my eyes.

"*Now it's your turn to please me, princess.*"

Chapter Thirty-Three

Vale

Down in the cells, I paced back and forth. There was no way I could wait until the raid happened. It had to be now.

I couldn't let Jessica be taken away tomorrow, or there was a good chance I'd never see her again. El Alfa hadn't given away much information about where the girls would be sold to after they went to Antigua. She might end up in Russia, or China, or Brazil. There was no way to be sure where she would go after El Alfa had given her to the highest bidder. I only hoped that he would keep his hands off of her before I had the chance to rescue her.

A noise in the hallway made me stop pacing. A woman sobbing. I came out into the hall, closing the metal door behind me. It wasn't Jessica, though. It was her friend, in between two guards. There were handprints on her hips. A flare of anger made adrenaline pump through my veins.

"Finishing up for the night?" one of the guards asked.

"Yeah," I said. "Is El Alfa done with the girls?"

"Done with this one," the second guard said. He dragged Jessica's friend into her cell and began putting the chain back through the loops.

"And the other one?" My mouth was dry, but I was calm. I came forward and planted myself in the doorway, between them.

They weren't careful with their weapons. The first

guard had put his machine gun against the wall before locking up Jessica's friend. He was still messing with the chain lock. Already, the plan was forming in my mind.

"Oh, he's still having fun with that one," the guard said, laughing. My blood boiled and I struggled to maintain composure. The guard outside was tired, yawning. His hands were nowhere near his gun.

Do it. Do it now.

I tried to think rationally, but I couldn't. The idea of Jessica up there at the hands of El Alfa… it was too much for me to handle.

I turned away from the doorway, my arms coming up lightning-quick. I grabbed the guard in the hallway and smashed his head against the stone wall. He grunted once and slumped down to the floor, his gun clattering to the ground behind him.

"Hey, what's going on out there?" the other guard asked. As he leaned out into the hall, I grabbed his head and twisted. Dumb fuck. He hadn't even bothered to pick up his gun.

Then the girl screamed.

I stepped across the body of the guard and clapped a hand over her mouth. She shrieked against my palm.

"Shh, shh," I said, panic rising in me. I hadn't counted on her making a scene, but I could hear footsteps coming down the stairs already. "Be quiet!"

She screamed again against my hand. There wasn't much time. Letting her scream, I darted back into the hallway and dragged both guards into Jessica's room. Closing the door, I was back in the hall as another guard came down the bottom step, holding his gun.

I pretended to zip up my pants.

"Everything okay?" he asked.

"Bitch isn't trained properly," I said, shrugging in the direction of the cell where Jessica's friend was still screaming. "El Alfa told me to try with her, but she's crazy."

"Oh, that one doesn't listen at all," the guard said, peeking into the cell. He slung his gun over his shoulder to pull the door shut. The screams were muffled.

"Hey, do you know where—"

The man's neck snapped like celery. Again the darkness rose inside of me as I dragged his body into Jessica's cell with the others.

Two dead. One unconscious. I snapped cuffs on the unconscious man and left him chained up in there with the others. I took one of the machine guns and tucked the extra ammo into my back pocket. They each had pistols and knives. I debated for only a moment before taking one of the knives and tucking it into my belt. The pistols I left in another empty cell.

My motions were quick, automatic. My shirt was still bloody from the cut Jessica had given me, but I didn't feel hurt at all.

I had a new mission now.

At the top of the stairs, I looked left, then right, and stopped dead.

Valentina was standing there in the hallway, right in front of me. Her eyes tracked the gun on my back.

"Hello, Vale," she said.

Fuck. I'd hoped to be able to do this mission alone.

"Hey, Valentina," I said, hefting the gun on its strap.

"You get promoted?" she said, eyeing me suspiciously.

"Something like that," I said.

She stood with her hands on her hips. I tried desperately not to notice her nipples perking through the gauze dress she was wearing.

"What exactly do you think you're doing?"

I had to trust her. There was no way around it. I hated being dependent on anyone, especially during a mission that had gotten as fucked up as it already had. But she was the only person in the house who knew who I was, and I had to trust her.

"The two guards downstairs are dead."

Her eyes went wide with the realization of what I was saying.

"Dead?" At least she had the decency to whisper.

"I killed them. And one more, I don't know what post he came from." It could have been one of the perimeter guards, I guessed.

"But the raid isn't for another two days!"

So she knew about the raid. I took a deep breath and pulled her into the stairwell so that we wouldn't be caught while I tried to explain.

"I can't wait for the raid," I said.

"Why the fuck not?" She sounded pissed, and I didn't know why, but it wasn't helping.

"El Alfa was going to ship out the girls tomorrow," I said. "We can't wait until the raid."

"There are always more girls," Valentina hissed. "You can't fuck up the timeline. They told us to wait for the raid."

I frowned.

"I can't let them go."

She leaned toward me, fire in her eyes.

"Stop playing savior, or you're going to get yourself killed! Do you know how many guards there are in this compound?"

I did know. I'd counted.

"Eight on the outside perimeter. Seven now. Ten more asleep. And three downstairs. They're dead or unconscious."

"And David."

"And David." I'd forgotten about the little bastard. He didn't have perimeter duty like the other guards.

"And El Alfa."

"I'm going to kill him right now. Then I'll clean up the rest."

"With what? A gun? You'll raise the whole house!"

"I have a knife."

"And a machine gun?"

I couldn't stand any more of her objections. With every second ticking away, Jessica was more likely to be hurt by El Alfa.

"That's just in case. Listen to me. All the girls upstairs, can you round them up and get them to a safe spot?"

"There isn't anywhere safe in here."

"There's an escape route in El Alfa's room."

Valentina sighed, but nodded. I said a quick thanks in my head. I needed her help. I hated needing anything from a woman.

"I know about it. But only he can access the door."

"We'll see about that," I said. "Get them gathered together and ready to go when I say so."

"I can't tell the girls what's going on."

"Why not?"

"Look," she said, as though she was explaining things to an idiot. "Some of the girls are loyal to the guards who train them."

"What?"

"They've been brainwashed. I wouldn't risk my life to save them. You shouldn't either. This is a crazy plan." She leaned out back into the hallway and darted a glance around, making sure there was nobody there.

"What about the girls in the cells?" I asked. I was sweating down my neck trying to get Valentina to agree with me. Jessica needed my help *NOW*!

"What about them?" she asked.

"If anyone knows what's going on, they'll be the first ones killed."

Now Valentina looked more than upset with me. She crossed her arms.

"They told me you were in control of this mission," she said carefully, slowly. "Your job is to kill El Alfa. Not save a bunch of slaves."

"I can do both."

"Oh? Really?"

"Really."

"There's no saving these girls now. Kill El Alfa, and you'll save all the ones who'd come after."

"I'll do that too," I said. But I was thinking about Jessica. I wasn't going to abandon her. But if I was going to save her and kill El Alfa early, I wouldn't be able to do it myself. I took Valentina's hand, desperation clutching my fingers tight around hers.

"Valentina, I need your help."

She blinked. Her mouth opened as if she was going to say something, then closed again. She looked irritated beyond belief, and a little bit scared. For the first time, I wondered if maybe she wasn't right.

Well, it was too late now.

I put a hand on her arm, and she looked up at me. I was desperate to get upstairs. I didn't know what El Alfa was doing with Jessica, but if the guards were right, I shouldn't spend a second more down here. I needed Valentina to be on my side before I went, though.

"Imagine if it was you down there," I said, letting my fear start to show. "Imagine if—"

"I don't have to imagine," she snapped. "I've gone through their training."

"Then help me save the rest of the girls from it."

She was silent.

"Please," I said. I was terrible at begging. Before, I'd always managed to get the job done myself. But I couldn't do that now. Not with Jessica's life on the line. I knew that I was putting Valentina at risk by including her in this mission, but there was nothing else I could think of that would save the innocent girls in those cells.

"Alright," she said finally. "What do you want me to do?"

I realized as I let my breath out that I'd been holding it in.

"Stand here. Take this knife. If any guard tries to go down the stairs, kill them."

"Kill them? How?"

The sound of footsteps coming down the side hall made both of us tense. Valentina ducked her head into the hall, then back quickly. Her face was pale.

"It's one of the outside perimeter guards," she whispered.

Looking up at the light above us, I had an idea. I wasn't sure if it would work, but it was the best shot we had.

"Stay here," I said, pushing her back into the shadows of the stairwell and to the side. I reached up and unscrewed the light bulb until it flickered out. The bulb was hot, and I swore as I pulled my fingers away, already burned pink.

I palmed the knife in my good hand and stepped out into the hallway.

The guard sidled up to me, caution on his face. Maybe he was wondering where his replacement was. His machine gun was already in his hands. A little better prepared than the other guards, but I hoped that wouldn't matter.

I wasn't going to shoot him. That would attract attention, and I didn't want any more of that.

"What's going on?" he asked.

"I think there's something wrong with this light," I said, pointing up. He looked up at the dim bulb, and I sliced the blade across his neck and stepped aside.

Blood sprayed out the front of the cut into the stairwell. He was still gurgling as I shoved him down the stairs, into the darkness. You couldn't see any more of him.

"Just like that," I said. I turned the knife around and held it up to her, praying she would take it. Jessica was in danger, and I needed to get to her now. "Can you do that?"

"I think I can do that," Valentina said, taking the knife from me and giving me, finally, an amused smile.

Chapter Thirty-Four

Jessica

"What other tricks has your trainer taught you?"

El Alfa circled around me, his hand hovering over the table full of whips and knives. I swallowed hard. I was still locked up by the collar, and I didn't think I'd be able to fight against him while I was still tied up. He could stay out of my grasp, and use any of the weapons against me. It was almost worse than having my hands tied.

"Well?"

My eyes came back to his. Dark, evil eyes.

"Lots of tricks," I said, racking my brain for an idea, _any_ idea. I'd read so many books that had crazy sex in them, but now my mind was blank.

"Good," he said. He reached the end of the table without picking up any of the weapons. Thank God for small favors. Now if only I could distract him so that he didn't need to use them…

My collar felt tight around my throat. It was hard to breathe. The chain hung heavy and pulled at my neck.

"Yes, lots of tricks," I repeated. My mouth was like cotton.

"Show me."

Oh, God. I had to do something. I thought of where Vale had first met me. The idea came to my mind in a flash.

"He likes me to dance," I said, making up the lie as I spoke the sentence. It was a good idea, I realized.

"Dance?"

"Yes," I said, enthusiasm coming into my voice. "If you unchain me, I can dance for you."

He eyed me suspiciously. I was being too enthusiastic, I realized. I dulled my face, putting on a blank, stupid expression.

"I like to dance," I offered up, pretending to be a stupid submissive girl. "I'll give you a good dance. A lap dance. You understand, a lap dance?" I patted my thighs.

The suspicion dropped away from his eyes. He thought I was stupid. He thought *I* thought he was stupid. Neither was true, but as long as I could keep him from being suspicious, I had a better chance of getting away.

"Yes, a lap dance. That sounds... nice," he said. He undid the lock, and I felt the chain swing away. The collar was still around my neck, but I wasn't chained anymore.

All I wanted to do was keep his attention occupied. I dreaded the thought of him touching me sexually. If I danced for him, though, I was only postponing the inevitable. Well, I'd try to postpone it as long as possible. He might fall asleep.

At least April was safe for now. I took some comfort in that.

Turning away from me, El Alfa headed to the bar. I edged closer to the table, trying to see if there was a weapon there that I could use on him. Before I could get close enough to grab anything, though, he turned around. I put on a simpering smile.

"Where do you want me to dance?" I asked, in my most innocent voice.

Yes, this was the Jessica I'd been before. The good girl. Always ready to please. Ready to do anything you wanted. Out of the corner of my eye, I saw a knife at the edge of the table. A small blade, glinting shiny and sharp. If I got the chance—

"There," he said, pointing toward a couch. I went over and sat obediently on the arm of the couch, my legs crossed. Good girl.

El Alfa pressed a button at the bar. Music started up, an intense pounding beat like the one that had been playing at his club. He poured himself a drink. I stood up and began to sway.

How the hell had I danced before? I didn't remember a single move. But if he was starting to drink again, hopefully that wouldn't matter.

He came over and I started dancing, gyrating my hips smoothly. My hands came up my sides, dragging along my curves. I didn't know exactly what you were supposed to do with your hands while dancing, and I wasn't confident enough to wave them around wildly.

"Come here," I said, and took his hand, leading him to the couch and gesturing for him to sit down. I don't know if it was because he was still somewhat drunk, but he let me push him down on the couch.

"Yes, dance," El Alfa said, taking a sip of his drink and putting it down on the arm of the couch. I let him touch my hips as I dipped down, swaying over his lap. Christ, I wish I had learned how to dance before this.

El Alfa didn't seem disappointed with my dancing, though. He slapped at my ass with a lazy hand and watched with mild interest as I squirmed and spun in front of him. Whenever his attention seemed to wane, I turned around and ground my hips against his lap. I didn't want him to get bored with watching, because then he'd want to do more. At the same time, I didn't want to keep him awake. It was an impossible situation.

The couch was facing away from the door, and every once in a while, I let my eyes drift over. If only he would fall asleep… I could kill him and escape out of the door.

His eyelids looked like they were drooping, but his cock wasn't. His obvious arousal was going to keep him awake until he was able to get more from me. He slapped my ass again, and the sound echoed. He stretched in his seat.

I was bending over in front of him when I heard the zip of his pants. I froze.

"Now take off those panties," he growled.

Fear dripped down the back of my spine. I forced myself to take a deep breath and stand back up slowly.

"But…but I'm a virgin," I said, turning around and putting on a pouting face. I didn't have to work to make my lip tremble. "Don't you want to keep me pure?"

The table was only a few feet away. I could leap over him and maybe, *maybe*, I would be able to get to the knives before he did. Even then, how was I supposed to know how to fight?

"Is that what you think?" he said. He moistened his lips.

"Well… maybe?" I was playing dumb.

"Come here," he said. "Lean closer."

I leaned closer, letting my breasts swing out in front of me. I thought of Vale and how I'd felt his length between my breasts. Would El Alfa do that? I shuddered to think about it.

And then my mind went back further, to what Vale had said about knives.

About the best way to kill someone.

El Alfa slapped me. The sting of the slap ratcheted through my head and I recoiled instinctively. His fingers, though, hooked under my collar, and he pulled me close. My eyes burned with stinging tears from the slap, but I blinked them away.

"Stupid bitch," he hissed.

My first thought was that he was reading my mind, but I realized that I'd already offended him.

"Your job isn't to think, girl," he spat at me. "This is my house. I can do what I want to. Understand?"

I nodded my head. He shook me by the collar harder, making my teeth knock together.

"Understand?"

"Yes!" I cried out, shaken by the blow. "Yes, I understand."

"Now. Take off your panties."

I swallowed as El Alfa let go of my collar, sending me reeling backwards. I struggled to stand, and slipped my fingers under my panties. My hands were trembling.

This. This was how I was going to lose my virginity. Here, in the bedroom of a sex slaver, without any dignity left. All of my skin turned cold, numb, and I started to pull my panties down.

Then my eyes lifted, and I saw him. The door was open, and Vale was standing right there.

With a gun in his hand.

Chapter Thirty-Five

Vale

I circled the compound, heading towards El Alfa's room. The perimeter guards were all outside; I wasn't sure when their shifts would end. I had to assume that someone would raise the alarm sooner rather than later, but I had no way of knowing. And Valentina was the only one standing watch. It was against my nature to trust anyone, let alone a woman I knew was capable of lying, and lying well.

But there was no way around it.

There was one guard standing outside El Alfa's room. I raised a hand in a short wave. Before the man could wave back, my hand had turned into a fist across his jaw. He went down cold, and I caught him before he could hit the floor.

I looked around for a place to put his unconscious body. There was nothing around. I tugged him next to one of the square planters near El Alfa's room and took his pistol, tucking it into the back of my pants.

Now I had two guns.

I pushed open El Alfa's door quickly but quietly. I knew that if he was going to see the door open, it was better off doing it fast. But he didn't see me.

Jessica did.

I froze as her eyes lifted up and fixed on the machine gun in my hand. Her collar was still on, but she wasn't chained up. No, she was nearly naked, straddling El Alfa, her hands pulling down at her panties.

My heart rose into my throat. Would she scream? Would she give me away? I had no idea if she understood what it was I was doing. There had been no time to tell her—

Her eyes flashed back down to El Alfa. He must have seen something in her eyes, a flash of fear. He sat up on the couch and started to turn his head. She ran both of her hands through his hair, pressing her breasts into his face to distract him.

I could have shot him right then and there, but I would be giving everything away with the noise. My best chance was a knife, but I'd left my knife with Valentina.

The table between us was covered in instruments of torture. Some of them were knives.

I knew I had to move quickly. I stepped forward with the gun, hoping to grab a knife so that the kill would be quiet.

He had some instinct, though. As I moved toward him, I knew why he called himself invincible. He couldn't have seen me, or heard me. It was another sense that made him jump up suddenly, spinning up from the couch before I could reach him.

"Stop."

"*Ahhhh!*"

He had Jessica in front of him. His hand yanked her collar hard, and twisted. She put both hands up to her neck, but it was useless. He had her dangling by the throat right in front of him. She choked on her scream.

"Let her go," I said.

"Why? So you can get a clear view to shoot me?"

He tugged at her collar harder. Her face was red. The temples on her veins throbbed.

"Put down the gun," El Alfa said. "Put down the gun or she dies."

"Let her go."

"Really? I thought you were a better man than this. To kill a girl—"

"Let her go."

He smiled. All the while, Jessica's arms tugged uselessly at his arm. He continued to choke her. I trembled. I had my orders—

—*Kill El Alfa*—

—and I wasn't about to give up this chance, no matter what happened to me or Jessica. I cocked the gun. Sweat tickled the back of my neck.

"One last chance," I said.

"Put it down."

The voice came from behind me. I felt the muzzle of a gun against my temple first, and then the man came into view.

Shit.

David.

"Vale, you've made a very bad mistake."

"David," I said, casting around for a way to get out of this situation, "don't do this."

"A very, *very* bad mistake," he repeated.

My glance fell on Jessica. She was still choking under El Alfa's grip.

"I'm taking over," I said. I would bluster my way through this. It was the last thing I could do. "I'm taking over this whole place. You can join me, David. We can be partners—"

"I don't think so."

"Wait. Think about it," I said. Sweat beaded on my

upper lip. I hoped he didn't see it. I was always in control. Always. And now, because of Jessica, I wasn't.

"I don't need to think about it, Vale," David said. I felt the gun press into the back of my head harder.

My eyes went wide as I took in everything in front of me. This—this awful scene—would be the last thing I ever saw. The electric torches on the wall. The disheveled bed. The chains hanging from the ceiling above El Alfa and Jessica. And the table, full of whips and knives and—

The knives. I frowned. There was something different about the way the knives were placed. When I'd come in, they had been lined up almost to the edge. I tilted my head. No. There wasn't anything different. I was going crazy.

David was still speaking behind me.

"There's no reason to go against El Alfa. I have thought about it. Put the gun down, Vale. You're not going to shoot anyway. Not with the girl in the way."

"Once he's dead," I said, my voice belying my lack of confidence. "David, if you join me—"

"You don't understand."

David walked around me. The muzzle of the gun trailed along my temple up to my forehead, where it rested. A grin crept across David's face. I looked at him, and then El Alfa. Then back to him.

And now I saw the resemblance. It came like a jolt to my system. They had the same nose, the same facial structure. If David hadn't been so sunburned, I might have seen it right away.

"He's…he's your father?" My arm trembled.

David nodded, his eyes seething.

"There is no takeover. You're an idiot to try. Put the

gun down."

Then it was over. I was outnumbered, and David was right. I couldn't shoot El Alfa, not when a twitch of his arm would mean shooting Jessica instead.

"Okay," I said, racking my brain for another plan. There was nothing. "Okay."

I put the gun down slowly, letting it click to the tile floor. David kicked it away to El Alfa, who picked it up. And then I stood back up, raising my hands in the air in a gesture of surrender.

The mission was over.

I had failed.

Chapter Thirty-Six

Jessica

David kicked Vale's gun away from him, and I saw him wince as he raised his hands in the air. My breath hitched even as El Alfa tugged on my collar, straining forward. He picked Vale's gun off the ground and hefted it in his meaty hands.

Surrender? No. He couldn't surrender! Vale was the one who was supposed to rescue me. He was the one who had promised that I wouldn't be a prisoner forever. He couldn't surrender. He couldn't!

There was only one way I could think to escape now. I hoped that it would work. If not, I would die trying.

El Alfa let his hand open up, and I gasped hot air. David grinned, his free hand scratching at the side of his neck.

I couldn't believe the truth—that David was El Alfa's son from one of the slaves in this house. How could anyone live with that family history behind them? How could he still keep doing this to girls when his own mother had been one of the prisoners?

"Son, you have done well. Let me give you a present."

El Alfa shoved me forward, and I stumbled halfway across the room, dropping to my knees with a hoarse cry.

"What, one of the whores?"

"This one's a virgin."

I saw the glint in his eye as he caught me by the arm and pulled me up to examine my body. I bit my lip, letting the fear show in my expression. My hands pressed tight against the sides of my body. Desire flared across his face.

"Kneel."

I bent down. He was unzipping his fly already, pulling down his pants. So eager.

So eager, in fact, that he didn't see the knife I was holding until it was too late.

Vale's lesson hadn't gone unheard. I remembered everything he had said about the easiest way to kill. And right now, there was one place that was accessible.

The femoral artery.

With a quick motion, I slid my blade into his leg and out. For a horrible second, I thought that it hadn't worked. David gripped my shoulder. He gasped, taking in a scraggly breath of air.

"Father—" he whispered.

Then the blood seemed to be everywhere, a flood of it, coating my legs even as I pulled away. He looked down at me, as though astonished I could have done such a thing. I was equally shocked. Then his face went pale, pale white, and he fell forward.

"David?"

El Alfa's voice boomed out from behind me.

"*David!*"

Chapter Thirty-Seven

Vale

I got to El Alfa just as he was aiming the gun. My hand came down on his arm and the shot rang out. I felt the bone break under my fist and I thought I had gotten to him in time. His hand opened and the gun began to fall.

"Ah!" he cried.

I caught the gun in mid-air and whipped it across El Alfa's jaw. He spun away, falling down onto the ground. His palms were slick with blood as he pushed himself up to look at me.

"Kneel," I said.

His arms trembled, and he glared at me with hatred burning in his eyes.

"You can't—"

Those were his last words. Then his face exploded with the shot. The gun was so close that I bet he smelled the gunpowder before his nose got blown off of his skull.

The shot echoed in my ears. But there wasn't even a hint of darkness when I killed him. No. This was a clean kill, the cleanest kill I'd ever had.

Emotionally, anyway.

Physically, his head was nothing but a mangled mess of blood and bone.

He slumped over, his neck still gushing blood onto the elegant tile floor. I straightened up, tucking the gun into my waistband.

"*Vale.*"

I turned to see Jessica falling forward. She stumbled onto the ground, clutching at her side.

My heart went cold. *No.*

"Jessica!"

I was at her side in an instant. There was a bullet hole in her side. I hadn't gotten to him in time. He had shot her.

The bastard. I wanted to kill him all over again. Anger and fear splintered through my body.

"Jessica, are you alright?"

She was pale.

"I—I don't know. I think so."

The bullet had hit her in the side. I saw the exit wound at the front, seeping blood. I put my hand over it. Her eyes fixed on something behind me.

"The door!"

The door banged open. I twisted my arm back and pulled out the gun, ready to shoot, but it was only Valentina. There was blood on the hem of her gauze dress. She stared past me, at El Alfa, agog.

"He's... he's dead?" she asked.

"Yeah," I said. My attention was on Jessica's side, where the wound under my hand was still leaking blood. I applied pressure, and she winced but didn't cry out. "We have to go."

"We heard the shot downstairs," Valentina said.

"Are the girls ready?" I asked.

"Yes," she said. "They're here."

"We'll have to hurry. Jessica—" I motioned to her wound. Emotion choked my throat. I'd never been one to have my feelings get in the way of words, but this time was different. I couldn't believe that I had let her get shot.

YOURS

"Go," Valentina said.

I set my shoulders square and swallowed back all of my anger and fear. Control. *Focus.* Immediately the plan came back into my mind. The door. Then escape.

I had a mission. It wasn't over. I could do this. I *had* to do this.

I set Jessica down and went back to El Alfa. I pulled his now-faceless body across the room.

"What are you doing?" Jessica asked.

"Getting us out of here."

I yanked El Alfa's arm up and pushed his thumb against the keypad. The metal door slid open.

Valentina reappeared in the doorway.

"Hurry," I yelled. It was too late to avoid raising an alarm. The guards would be here soon. The only chance we had was to disappear before they could figure out what had happened.

The girls were already running across the room to the open door. Valentina was hurrying them through. There were so many of them—fourteen girls in total. One of them stopped and stared at me. Jessica's friend, I realized.

"Go!" I cried. She ran through the open door and into the tunnel after the line of girls. Valentina followed, and then only Jessica and I were left.

I knelt down to Jessica's side, handing her the pistol.

"Take the gun," I said.

"What?" she asked weakly. "What are you—"

"Just take it."

I could hear the sounds of footsteps. The perimeter guards, coming back inside. We had to get out of there.

I picked up Jessica with both arms. She was bleeding from her back, the blood making her slippery to hold.

"It's alright," I said. "You're going to be alright."

She nodded her head, a slow weak nod.

"Let's go."

I crossed the room to the open door. Valentina was shooing the last of the girls through the tunnel. I didn't ask if any of them had been left behind. I knew that we had lost some of them. Some of them would have chosen to stay. Brainwashed, maybe, or just helpless. But we would get out of here. We would be okay. I stepped through the doorway into the dim corridor.

BANG!

The shot deafened me in my left ear. At first, confused, I thought that Jessica had shot me. I stumbled forward into the tunnel, clasping her tightly.

Then I realized that Jessica had shot the gun. But not at me. The gun was aimed into El Alfa's room behind us. I turned to see one of the guards sinking to his knees.

"Good shot," I said, as the metal door slid across our vision and erased the scene completely.

We hurried down the tunnel. Behind us, a dull banging echoed down the stairs. The guards were trying to get through the door. I could only hope that El Alfa's door would hold them off for a while.

I had no idea where I was going, and the electric torches were dim on the stone steps. Minutes passed that seemed like hours, as we made our way down through the stone. It was only after the last bend of the tunnel opened up that I could see.

We were outside. The moon was full, and it sparkled over the ocean water. The waves reflected the shimmering stars above. At any other time, the view would have been beautiful. Romantic. I paused, inhaling salt air as I caught my breath. Jessica's arms hung around my neck. Her breathing was shallow.

"Over here!" Valentina cried.

I looked up to see the girls wading into the water. Their white gauze dresses pooled around their waists as they edged out into the ocean. At the end of a rock jetty, two motorboats were tied up, waiting to take us home.

Chapter Thirty-Eight

Jessica

"Jessica? Sweetie?"

I blinked into fluorescent white light. White light. White curtains. I was in a hospital. There was a steady beeping noise coming from behind. My eyes focused on the blur hovering over me and the image resolved into my mother's face.

"Jessica?"

I lifted my head, turning it from side to side. The blurs were all faces. My mother. My father. Another woman at the foot of the bed, holding a clipboard. Two more men sitting in chairs, in dark uniforms.

"Don't move too quickly," the first woman said. Was she a doctor? A nurse? I didn't care. I craned my neck, but I couldn't see Vale.

"Where is he?" I asked.

The beeps came faster behind me. I pulled myself upright, ignoring the tubes that were taped to my arms.

"Jessica," my mother said, "It's alright. We're here."

"Where is he?"

Panic rushed over me as I lifted up my arms. I couldn't move—there were IVs in both of my wrists. I was tied.

"Your father's right here."

"Not him," I said, shaking my head as though that would get rid of the dizziness. *"Vale."*

"Who are you talking about?" my mom asked, a

worried look on her face.

"Vale," I repeated, trying to keep calm.

The breaths I drew were hotter and hotter. I pulled the sheet back and examined the tubing. There must be a way to get the IV out. I didn't want to stay here.

"Jessica, calm down," the woman said. "You're going to be alright, but you have a lot of injuries."

"Where's Vale?"

I tossed back the sheet to see what they had done to me. Under the sheet, my legs were pale white. There was a white bandage across my stomach. I dropped the IV tube and touched the bandage. A dull pain shot through my stomach and I clenched my eyes shut.

One of the men in dark uniforms stood up. A badge. Police. His eyebrows were like dark caterpillars frowning across his face. I thought of El Alfa, and my stomach revolted, turning over inside of me.

"Where is he? Is he not here? Is he okay?"

The air in the room felt like it was closing in on me. I didn't know why, but I needed to see Vale. It felt wrong to be sitting here without him.

"Please," the doctor said. "She needs rest. Jessica, don't get too excited."

I swallowed hard and made myself lean back into the hospital bed. Surely the policemen would know about him.

"Vale," I said. "I didn't know his last name. He was working for the police."

The two policemen looked at each other. I could tell they thought I was crazy. I struggled not to tear the IV tubes out and make a scene. They had to take me seriously.

"Where is he?" I asked, as slowly and calmly as I could make myself speak.

"Vale, you said?"

"Yes. His name is Vale." I gritted my teeth as the second policeman pulled out his phone and began tapping away.

"What did he look like?" the first cop asked.

"The man who brought you in?"

"Yes!" I turned to the woman doctor who had just spoken. "Did you see him?"

The doctor looked nervous to be the center of attention. She held her clipboard tightly in both her hands.

"He was the one who carried you into the emergency room. Tall guy, lots of—ah, lots of muscles, right?"

"Right," I said, my heartbeat slowing only slightly. "And blue eyes." For some reason, I thought that it was important to tell them. "Light blue eyes. Like ice."

"We didn't get his information," the doctor explained to the cops. "I think he left before anyone asked him for an ID. If you want, we can get you the security footage—"

"Yeah, that'd be great," the first policeman said.

The second policeman was staring at me with suspicious eyes, his arms crossed. I pressed my lips together. What if Vale wasn't with the police after all? Would they arrest him?

"Your friend told us this crazy story about a kidnapping ring. I'd like to ask you—"

"April?" I sat up instantly, my heart pounding. "Is she okay? Is she—"

"She's fine. A bit bruised, and—well, if her story is true, you know what happened to her."

"Y—yes," I said, replaying the horrible scene in my head. "It's true."

"We'd like to ask you a few questions, if you don't

mind," the first policeman said. "Take a statement."

"She just woke up!" my mom interjected.

"Really, officers," my dad chimed in. "Is this necessary right now?"

"With what we've heard so far from her friend, yes, it is necessary," the second policeman said. "I'm sorry, but her friend reports that this man—the one who you claim brought you in—shot and killed her boyfriend."

My mom wrung her hands against her chest. I could only blink.

James. It felt like so long ago. So, so long ago.

"And from what I'm hearing, there seems to be a connection between you and this man—ah, Vale," the cop continued. "You have to understand that these events could implicate you in the case that…"

He kept talking, but there was a rush of blood in my head and I was dizzy. My mom was standing up and yelling at the cop, and then both of them were yelling, and my dad was standing back silently like he always did during a fight. It was so loud, and the beeping behind my bed grew louder and louder. I pressed my hands to my ears but it didn't keep out the sound.

"She's just been *kidnapped*—"

Beep.

"Ma'am, if there's any way she can identify the suspect—"

Beep.

"Kidnapped! And her friend was raped! And you want to—"

Beep.

The door opened. Everybody stopped talking and turned to the man who was now standing in the doorway.

He was tall, muscular, and had short-cropped dark hair. His suit was rumpled.

For a moment, there was silence except for the steady, quick beeping of the machines.

"Is that him?" Both policemen turned to me. I shook my head slowly. I didn't know who this man was. I'd never seen him before in my life.

"Hey, everyone," the man said, digging in his pocket. He pulled out a badge and flashed it toward the cops. "FBI."

"FBI?"

"You can go. We've got this covered."

"*Excuse* me," the second policeman said, sarcasm dripping from his lips. "We were about to question the witness."

The dark-haired man laughed with a confidence that cut through all of the tension in the room. It was clear that the police were no longer in charge. This guy was in charge. Whoever he was.

"Get out," he said.

"But it's our case—"

"The city of San Diego has zero jurisdiction here," the man said, his smile disappearing as quickly as it had come. "This is an *international* crime in a *federal* case that we've been tracking for almost a decade now."

"So?"

"So?" He peered at the cops. "So you two can fuck along now."

The two policemen stood agape for a moment. Then the second policeman scoffed and turned on his heel. The first cop followed him out.

"May I speak with Jessica alone?" the man asked my

parents.

"I don't—"

"It's okay, mom," I said quickly. There was something about this man that reminded me of Vale. At the very least, he seemed like he might know what was going on. "It's alright. Let me talk with him."

My mother pinched her lips together and left arm in arm with my father. The doctor went out behind them, closing the hospital door. Then it was just me and the man who claimed to be with the FBI.

He pulled up a chair next to my hospital bed and sat down casually.

"My name is Ten," the man said.

"Ten?"

"Yeah. Weird name, huh?" He chuckled nervously. I already liked him. The past few weeks had made me question my instincts, but in the end I knew that I could trust myself. And that meant trusting him.

"Did you want to ask me about what happened?" I asked. "About the kidnapping?"

"Maybe later. Right now I want to make sure you're okay. And that you don't tell anyone else about Vale."

My mouth went dry.

"You know him?"

"Yes."

"Where is he?"

"I'm sorry. I can't tell you that."

"But…but…" I stammered.

"He's on another mission right now," Ten said. "He's going to have to lay low for a while. He told me to let you know that."

I swallowed hard.

"Will he—will I ever see him again?"

"That's what I came here to find out. Vale told me that he had to do some terrible things in Mexico. To your friend, and also to you."

My skin flushed hot as I thought about everything Vale had done to me.

"I want to let you know that he was under orders— my orders." The man's mouth pinched together in contrition. "I'm just as much at fault for your friend's death as he is."

Tears slid down my cheeks. I wasn't crying, but the tears were still there. I thought of James. I remembered the way Vale had looked after he pulled the trigger. A dead man's eyes.

Do you think if I hadn't shot him, he would still be alive?

"He wasn't sure you would want to hear from him again," Ten said, quickly moving on. "If that's the case, then you can just say the word."

"And… and if not?"

Ten smiled gently.

"I can give him your contact information if you want him to have it."

"I do," I blurted out. "I—I want to thank him. For saving me."

"Of course," Ten said. "Here."

He handed me a notepad. I wrote down my cell phone number. It was hard to write clearly. For some reason, my hand was trembling.

"When will he be back?" I asked.

"I can't tell you that."

"Oh. Sure. Okay."

"But I'll be sure to give him your number as soon as

he's back in the country."

I nodded. The man stood up and straightened out his suit jacket. As he turned, I caught his arm.

"Wait," I said. "I have a question for you."

"Yeah?"

"Vale… he's a good guy, right?"

"A good guy?"

Ten's eyes dropped to mine and the world's weight seemed to be on his shoulders. He bit his lip, and I knew from his face that he wasn't going to lie to me. Finally he spoke.

"As far as I'm concerned," he said, "he's a goddamned hero."

A week passed, then another, then another. Impossibly, things around me returned to normal. The hospital released me after only a few days. My parents argued that I should move in with them, but I stayed in the apartment with April. She was the only one who could understand what I'd gone through. We talked about it a lot at first, then less after James' funeral, then not at all.

Everybody knew, but nobody wanted to talk about it. I didn't blame them. What do you say to someone who had survived all that I had? Better not to say anything at all. I shoved back all of my feelings and all of my hurt, and tried to pretend that I had moved on just like everybody else had seemed to.

I was on my laptop, registering for next semester's classes, when my phone rang. I picked it up without thinking.

"Hello?"

"Jessica?"

His voice hit me like a physical thing. All the air in the room seemed impossibly heavy. I sucked in a breath.

"Vale? Is that really you?"

"Sure is, darling. I hear you're doing better now."

I touched my stomach. The new scar was still puckered and red. I could feel it itching as the skin knitted together at my back and in the front, where the bullet had torn a hole.

"Y—yes. I'm fine. I'm okay."

"Are you?"

The concern in his voice was too much. All of a sudden, tears were streaming down my cheeks. I hadn't cried since James' funeral, but now, hearing his voice, it was like a floodgate had opened. I hiccupped back sobs as I struggled to speak.

"Vale, I can't—I'm sorry—I don't know why I'm being like this. I'm sorry!"

"It's okay," he said, as I stifled my sobs back with a tissue. "It's alright."

"I'm sorry," I kept repeating. "I'm sorry—"

"Jessica." Something in his voice made me snap to attention.

"Yes?"

"Please don't. You're not the one who should apologize. Look, if you don't want to talk to me, we don't have to—"

"No!" I nearly yelled it.

"No?"

"No," I said, calming myself. "No, I want to—I want

to talk. You're the only one I can talk to!"

"Me?" There was a note of disbelief in his voice.

"Yes! April doesn't want to bring it up ever, and all of my friends—when they see me, they look away. It's like I'm cursed, and nobody wants to talk to me because it'll rub off on them. Or they just don't know what to say to me. And my parents are even worse and I don't want to talk with them about it because nobody can understand, they just can't! And I've been having these dreams…"

I stopped myself.

"I'm sorry," I said, sniffling into the already-wet tissue. "I'm ranting. Can I—can we meet again, Vale?"

"You want to see me again?" Again, he sounded like he couldn't believe me.

"You're the only one who knows what I've been through. You… you saved me."

There was a silence on the other end.

"Sure," he said. "Yeah."

"When can we meet?"

Hope bloomed in my chest.

"Well, thing is, I'm in Guatemala right now."

"Guatemala?" Now it was my turn for disbelief.

"El Alfa was shipping to some other compounds out here. We just closed them down."

Relief flooded through me. I thought about what that man had said—that Vale was a hero. I believed it.

"That's—that's good."

"I'm not going to be able to go back to America for a while, I don't think," Vale said. "The West coast, anyway. I gotta stay away from anywhere El Alfa knows people. Knew people. It's dangerous."

"Oh. Okay." My voice caught on the last word.

He wasn't going to come to see me. Disappointment welled up, tearing my eyes up again. I blotted them out roughly. I was angry for being so sad. Angry for needing Vale.

It was a moment before I realized he was talking again.

"Why don't you come out here?"

There was a pause while I parsed his question. Go out there? To Guatemala? Before I could answer, he was talking again.

"If you don't want to, I completely understand. But—"

"I want to."

The words were out of my mouth before I realized it.

"You're sure?"

I smiled through my tears. I hadn't known what I needed until now. But hearing his voice made me realize that there was only one way for me to get past what had happened. And I needed Vale.

"Yes," I said. "I'm sure."

Chapter Thirty-Nine

Vale

I met her at the airport. She looked so fragile, but she smiled bravely. I followed her lead, hugging her back when she lifted her arms. The touch of her skin made my body twinge with desire, but I held back.

It took all of my willpower to hold back, but I held back. It was amazing to me that she was even here, that I could reach out and touch her. After the mission, I couldn't believe that she would ever want to see me again. I'd begun to think that it was for the best. So her deciding to come here to visit me took me by surprise.

"Where are we going?"

She looked nervously around at the crowds of people thronging out of the airport. I motioned her out to the curb. There was a silver sedan waiting for us outside.

"I thought we could go sailing. There's a hotel, if you'd rather not. Not that we'd stay in the same room. I could get you another room. I mean…"

I stopped myself. For some reason, having Jessica nearby turned me into a stammering fool. Without anyone around for me to pose for, I wasn't nearly as much of a badass. I caught her smiling at me, and I smiled back.

"Sailing?"

She arched an eyebrow at me.

"You're a sailor?"

I let out a sharp laugh. I'd never thought anyone would ever call me a sailor. I hated boats. But I'd been trying to get rid of my fears one at a time.

"I've been learning. It's fun, actually. Boats. They can be fun."

I opened the door and she climbed into the passenger's seat.

"You'll have to show me."

We didn't talk about anything serious at first. I pointed out the monkeys and pigs in the countryside. She chatted about the flight, and I told her bits and pieces about what I'd done in Guatemala after we'd escaped from El Alfa's compound.

It was only when we got to the dock that she quieted down. I led her down the rickety pier carefully, holding her arm to make sure she kept her balance. The boards were precariously laid, crooked and warped by the humidity, with gaps that yawed open, waiting to claim an ankle. She wound her way down the wooden steps and around to the end where the boat was tied.

"I'll take your suitcase," I said. She nodded silently, and silently took my hand. Hers was small and warm, cradled in my fingers. I helped her down onto the deck and she stumbled forward as a wave rocked the boat against the dock. I caught her around the waist and eased her down quickly to safety in the middle of the deck, where she could lean against the mast.

She looked around the boat, her palms pressed back against the mast to steady herself. It seemed incredible to me that she was here. I'd truly thought that the hospital would be the last time I saw her.

"This is a pretty sailboat," she said.

"It's a catamaran."

"What's the difference?"

"See the hulls?" I pointed to the long wooden hulls stretching out on either side of her past the mast. "There are two of them."

"Why?"

"It's more stable," I explained.

"So you won't tip us over as easily?" she asked, smiling mischievously.

"Exactly."

We sailed out from the edge of the coast. She laughed with glee the first time we crossed a boat wake, and the hull rocked up and down sharply, clapping against the murky green water. The rays of late afternoon were still hot on our faces, and she sat smiling on the deck, her face upturned to the bright sun, as I steered us out to the open sea.

The boat was stable, and she seemed stable too. Surprisingly stable, after everything that had happened. I didn't want to bring it up too soon, so I let the silence hang over us. It was a strangely comfortable silence, as though we'd known each other for much longer than we actually had. I lifted my head into the wind, reveling in the peacefulness of sailing. It was nice, really, as long as the waves weren't too strong. This boat was stable.

The water grew clear and blue as we headed towards a cluster of small islands just off the coast. The air here blew fresh and cool compared to the hot and humid inland. I thought Jessica was enjoying the sail, and I left her alone as I managed the wheel.

It was only when I'd turned into the middle of a reef and dropped the sails that I realized she was crying softly.

"Jessica?"

I set the anchor and quickly sat down next to her. I

put an arm around her and she drew close into me, crying, her hands limp in her lap.

"Jessica? Are you alright?"

"Yes," she said, sniffing once. She smiled through her tears. "I mean, no, but yes."

"No, but yes?" I smiled back at her gently. I didn't want to scare her. I didn't want to hurt her. I was so worried that she would turn around and disappear again. But she only leaned into my arm and laughed through her tears.

"I'm better now than any time in the past month or so. You're the first person to treat me normally, you know?"

I didn't know, but I nodded like I did. She continued, the tears dripping down all the way to her chin.

"Everybody else…they all look at me strange. They don't know what to say around me. They treat me like I have a disease, like I'm contagious. April doesn't want anything to do with me. It's like I'm reminding her of what happened just by being around. And my parents… well, they're my parents."

She wiped her hand across her wet cheeks. Stupidly, I fumbled for the right words.

"I'm sorry, Jessica. I can't tell you how sorry I am for everything that happened. For everything I did."

"For James? I know."

There. That was it. She would always remember that I'd killed her friend, no matter why. No matter what excuses I made for it.

"You did what you had to," she said. She looked up at me over tear-stained cheeks with a wry little smile. "How many women did you save here? In Guatemala?"

I blinked.

"Who told you about what I was doing here?"

"Your friend. Ten."

"Ten is not my friend," I corrected quickly. "He's my boss."

"He seems to like you a lot for just being your boss," Jessica said.

"Yeah, well. He's a good guy."

It was strange to me that, as much as I'd cursed his name in the past, I thought this was true. Ten *was* a good guy. He made me do his dirty work, yeah. But usually there was method behind his madness. And we had done a lot of good work, too.

"So how many?" she pressed.

"A lot," I admitted truthfully.

"How many did you save?"

This was a girl you couldn't fuck around with. I appreciated her bluntness.

"Thirty-four in Guatemala City."

She raised her eyebrows.

"And another twenty in Antigua."

"He said you were a hero," she said. She spoke so softly, I almost didn't hear the end of her sentence. It shocked me.

"What? No. I'm not—I do my job. I follow orders."

"Is that what you did in Tijuana?"

I tilted my head. Smart girl, too. I couldn't get anything by her. I hadn't followed any orders at El Alfa's compound. Ten had been furious with me, but only until I told him what I knew. It felt good to bring down something bigger than just one guy, but I hadn't done it alone.

"I'm not a hero," I said finally.

"You are," she said. She leaned into my arm. "You're my hero."

"Nah, Jess," I said, embarrassed.

"Vale?"

Her eyelashes were dark on her cheeks as she tilted her head back against my shoulder.

"Yeah?"

"When you came up to me and we started dancing, that was the craziest thing I'd ever done in my life."

I didn't know what she was driving at, so I stayed silent.

"But I've been wondering… I need to know… was any of it real?"

"Real?"

"I mean, did you… did you ever want me?"

Tears spilled over her cheeks as she looked up at me.

"Oh, Jessica." I hugged her closely with my arm, nuzzling the top of her head. Her hair smelled like coconut.

"It was all fake, wasn't it? El Alfa told you to do it, and you did—"

"No."

"You never wanted me at all—"

"That's not true."

"It isn't?"

I cradled her face in my hands and turned her so that she had to look at me. She sniffed, her eyes rimmed red with tears, putting on a brave face.

"You don't have to lie to me, Vale," she said, in a voice so soft and broken it made my heart ache. "Please don't lie…"

"Jessica, I'll never lie to you again. Do you believe me?"

Her lip quivered. She bit it and nodded her head.

"I wanted you the moment I saw you dancing in the middle of that crowd. That's—that's why El Alfa sent me after you."

"Why?"

"Because you were the first one to catch my eye. I always thought—I thought it was my fault you were there, because I was the one who chose you."

She was silent. I sat there, unsure of what to say. There was a tension between us, something rippling and dark under the surface, and I wasn't sure if it was a good idea to go too deep.

"Jessica?"

"Yes?"

"I'm sorry I ever lied to you. I'm sorry for everything that happened."

"It—it wasn't your fault," she said. Her voice trembled over the words.

"It doesn't matter whose fault it was. I take full responsibility for everything I did. I'll have that weight on my conscience forever. The only thing I can do is promise that I'll never lie to you. I'll never hurt you again. And if there's anything I can do for you, just tell me and I'll do it."

Her eyes closed over her tears and a silent sob wracked her body. I pressed my forehead against hers. She looked so small in my arms, so fragile. I would have killed a hundred El Alfas to save her again.

"Tell me what you want, Jess," I whispered. "Anything... anything you want."

The words were soft, so soft that I had to lean forward to catch them.

"I want... I want to be yours."

Chapter Forty

Jessica

For an awful second, I thought I had messed everything up. Vale looked down at me with such shock in his eyes that I thought he was going to turn around and jump overboard to swim a mile to shore. But then the look softened.

"Jessica, I didn't ask you here to…I…I don't want you to think you owe me anything."

I shook my head.

"It's not about that," I said.

"You're sure that you want this? You want _me_?"

He seemed so surprised. His reaction threw me. Most guys that handsome assumed that women wanted them. Vale seemed to be doing everything in his power to avoid that conclusion.

He looked off to the side of the boat and I let my gaze drift down his body. He was wearing a white buttoned shirt and casual khaki slacks. He was tanner, too, than he'd been in Mexico. I wondered if too much had changed. But I had come here for a reason, and I kept a hold of it in the front of my mind.

"Vale," I said, as clearly as I could, "I've never wanted anything else so badly."

Then his mouth was on mine, taking the breath from my lips in a kiss that was gentle at first, then more and more insistent. His arms drew me closer as he kissed me.

"Oh, Jessica."

I leaned into the kiss, deepening it. Every minute on the way here, I'd been terrified of what I'd find when I arrived. Vale hadn't been his real self in Mexico. I didn't know who he would be. I only had a thin hope that he was the kind of man that I thought he was, the kind of man I saw peeking out from under the façade back when I was locked up.

Feeling him touch again made me shiver with emotion. Yes, he'd done terrible things under order. But when I thought about what he'd done to me, it wasn't anything that made me angry, or upset. I was only angry at the real villains—El Alfa, David. And the real villains were all dead. We had killed them.

It was true. He was my hero. And when I thought about how he had touched me, about what he'd done to me… I could only wish for him to touch me again.

His mouth moved hesitantly down to my neck. I could feel him resisting with every touch, every heartbeat. His hands fluttered over my shoulders, down my arms. He didn't want to take me without my consent. He didn't realize he already had it.

As his lips pressed against my neck just under my ear, I took his hand and pulled it around my waist. My own hand drifted down, molding itself to his chest.

He looked into my eyes, and his gaze was a question. I answered it.

"More."

I leaned back and he lay me down against the thin cushion on top of the deck. The boat rocked slowly in the swell of the waves, tugging against the anchor.

"You're the most beautiful girl in the whole world," he said, with all sincerity. I didn't know what to say, so I

244

just laughed.

"And your laugh is the most beautiful laugh in the whole world."

The sun was starting to dip down to the horizon.

"Is that your normal pick up line?" I asked.

"I don't pick girls up," he said.

"No? Never?"

"Well… with my line of work…" he said, gesturing in the air. The reddish rays of the sun gleamed off of his tan skin. "It's hard to start a relationship."

"Right. Here I was thinking you don't pick up girls, you just kidnap them."

His shock quickly turned to amusement when he saw my joking expression.

"Sorry," I said, giving him a wry smile as I let my hand touch his shoulder.

"I'm not used to having girls joke with me," he said.

"It's alright. As long as you don't mind it from now on."

"Do you always joke around?"

"Not always. Just whenever I get swept up by a handsome kidnapper."

"You are the most beautiful girl I've ever kidnapped," he said suavely, joking right back at me.

A furious giggle rushed up inside of me and I pressed my fingers to my lips. I felt…not normal. That wasn't it. I felt *free*. Like the first time we'd crossed over the Mexican border. Only this time, freedom tasted a whole lot sweeter.

"Thanks," I said, not knowing how to make it mean more.

I grinned as he pulled me into another kiss. All of my hesitation vanished as his lips found mine and shocks of pleasure raced through my body. His mouth was hot, pressing insistent kisses against mine.

I'd never felt so safe. It was weird, I suppose. I should have been afraid of him. He was a killer, he admitted that much and more. He had done terrible things. But when his hands smoothed my dress down, cupping my hips in his large palms, I felt like nothing else in the world could touch me.

Here I was, floating in the middle of the ocean, and I felt completely free.

A rasp of his breath in my ear made me shiver. I kissed his neck, savoring the taste of ocean on his skin. His breath caught in his throat on the inhale. Despite his muscles, I could feel his arms trembling around me.

"God, Jessica, you don't know what you do to me."

"*Or,*" I said, another smile slinking up my face, "I know exactly what I'm doing to you. Even if I don't know what I'm doing at all."

His face shone with surprise and delight. And when he kissed me, I arched into him, letting his hands take me up by the hips. I could feel his cock through his pants, straining against the fabric. I knew he wanted me.

And this time, I was going to be able to let him take me.

He cradled me in his arms and leaned me back against the thin deck cushion. Underneath us, small waves slapped up along the side of the boat's hull. He pressed kiss after kiss on my mouth, my cheeks, my neck. He nibbled his way down to the straps of my dress and nibbled his way back up to my ear. Every touch of his, every graze of his fingers, sent electrical thrills through my body.

When he gave me a little bit of space, I gasped. The

air was cool and salty. The sun was almost to the edge of the world, and the other side of the sky was going dark.

I'd talked with April about losing my virginity, before we had ever even thought about taking a trip to Mexico. She'd told me that it wouldn't feel great the first time, that it would hurt a little. She told me that I really should just get it over with so that I could stop worrying about it, because there was no way that I would enjoy sex my first time.

Despite all this, I was so very glad that I had waited. In this moment, I knew that Vale was the only man I could trust enough to take me from virginity to the other side. I trusted him, as strange as it sounded, because I had seen hints of the real him peeking out in the days when I was locked up. I had seen who he really was. And now, now that he was opening up, everything I saw made me even more firm in my decision. Vale was the one.

I wasn't sure if I could ask him for what I wanted, though. I wet my lips and tried to think of a way to say what it was that I desired, but I couldn't. My whole body ached for him.

My fingers explored the edge of his white shirt. I stopped at the seam of his scar peeking out just under his collarbone.

He froze above me. I could almost hear our heartbeats pounding in the dimming ocean air.

"Vale?"

He took my fingers, picked them up from where they were touching his scar. He lifted my fingers to his lips and kissed them.

"This is… hard for me," he whispered.

"What?"

"Trusting you. I haven't been with anyone since after Jen tried to kill me. I tried, but I couldn't. It just didn't work. It was impossible for me to let someone in. But you…"

He trailed off, looking at my fingers. He bit his lip, uncertainty playing across his strong features.

"I can't hold back with you," he said finally. "I want you too much."

That was it. Relief flooded through me. I could ask him. I knew I could.

"Will you—will you tie me up, Vale?"

He raised his eyebrows. For a moment, I thought that I had gone too far, asked too much.

"Tie you up?"

"I like it. I mean, I didn't like being chained up as a prisoner, but when you were kissing me, and…" My words started to stammer as I thought about what else he'd done to me. "I mean, I liked being tied up when I was with you. Is that weird?"

I flushed as I spoke. My body was ready for him, my whole self was ready to throw myself into this, but I wasn't sure if I was asking the right thing.

"Not weird at all. Lots of people like that. But…"

"But?"

He brushed my hair away from my eyes and tilted my chin up so that I met his gaze.

"You have to promise me that if you feel uncomfortable, you'll let me know."

I nodded quickly.

"Of course."

"Is this something you've always wanted?"

I looked up at him. I hadn't expected his questions,

but now that he was asking them, it forced me to look inside myself deeper than I'd looked before. Why did I want this?

"Yes," I said slowly. "I didn't know before… I didn't know what I wanted. But there was always this…shadow over everything. I didn't want what other girls wanted. I didn't want a nice boyfriend who bought me drinks and flirted and met me at the door with a bunch of roses."

"A shadow?"

"I wanted something… darker. I tried not to want it. But I didn't know how to get rid of that shadow. I couldn't. And when you came along, I knew what it was that I'd been waiting for. Does that make any sense?"

I was hoping for any sort of reassurance. Vale's face was serious as he thought about what I'd said.

"I think we all have that. The shadow, I mean. There's part of everyone that's a little… darker than the rest. I know I have it, too. When I—"

He cut off mid-sentence, as though he didn't want to speak about it. I nodded. I thought I understood what he meant. He'd done dark things, to be sure. Maybe he would tell me about them later. I hoped he would. I didn't want him to hide anything else from me.

I heard his voice and refocused my attention.

"Jessica?"

I lifted my chin to meet his gaze. The ice-blue eyes that I had previously thought were cold had melted into gentleness. The only thing left in Vale's face was desire.

"Just to be absolutely sure—you're not doing this for me, are you?"

The question took me by surprise, and I laughed. With a burst of happiness, I pressed my hands on both of his cheeks.

"Oh, Vale!" I cried. "This… this is the first thing I've ever done for myself!"

I kissed him, and he met my desire with his own. Heat burned through my nerves as he lifted my dress over my head. The cool ocean air gave me goosebumps, but only for a moment. He kissed my shoulders, his palms warming my body as much from the inside as from without as he stroked my arms, my hips, my thighs.

He unhooked my bra, and I let it fall to the side of the deck. Letting my hips arch up, I helped him slide down my panties. They ended up in the same pile.

I was wet, so wet between my thighs. As Vale's eyes swept down appreciatively over my body, I couldn't stand it anymore. I reached for him to pull him to me.

"Vale," I murmured.

"Put out your wrists," he said. The order was firm and gentle, and I obeyed instantly. A thrill of fear mixed with my desire. I wanted this—there was nothing that I wanted more—but in that second I realized that I was giving something over completely, irrevocably. And that same thrill turned to a burning desire as he placed another kiss right in the hollow of my neck.

"Beautiful girl," he whispered.

His hands were strong, and he moved deftly with the rope from the front of the sailboat. He looped the rope around my wrists, binding them. With each loop, he pressed alternating kisses onto my palms. I shivered, more from desire than from the chill in the air.

My heart was already pounding. The thought of losing my virginity both thrilled and scared me. And with Vale, a man who had done so much to me already? For a brief moment, I thought of turning back, saying no. He would let me go immediately, I knew.

That itself comforted me. And when Vale gave my hand a little squeeze, the rest of my fear evaporated. This was all I wanted—to give myself to him completely. He was my hero and my savior, and the man I wanted more than anything in the world.

The sun was quickly fading below the horizon and the only light left was the bright lamp hanging from the main mast of the sailboat. As Vale tied the last loop, he pushed me back against the cushion. I followed him obediently, letting his hands lead me wherever he wanted. Instead of tying me with my arms stretched out on both sides, though, my arms were bound over my head. The rope ran from above my head to the front rail of the boat. When he tugged the rope tight, my arms tensed, but only a little.

"How is that?" he asked.

"Good." My voice was small, nervous. I knew what I wanted—at least, I thought I did—but now that it was really happening, I couldn't believe it.

Vale slid his hands down over my naked body. Where before he had tasted my skin with his eyes, he touched me, exploring the curves of my shoulder, my elbow, the crook of my knee just above my calf.

His hand paused at the scar on my belly.

"I did it to myself," I said. It was a confession I'd never made to anyone else, but with Vale I didn't want to hide anything. He knew already, part of it.

"You? You did this?" He didn't seem to believe me.

"I always tried to be so perfect," I explained unsteadily. "Everything on the outside was perfect. I just wanted to…to mess it up somehow."

His hand caressed my scar, and he leaned down to kiss it. His lips were hot, so hot against my skin. My body melted under his touch.

"Well, I'm sorry," he whispered.

"Sorry?"

"You didn't mess anything up. You're still completely perfect."

He smiled, and a rush of relief flooded through me. Although I had been worried, I shouldn't have been. Vale was the last man in the world who would judge me. The thought made my heart swell so big I thought it would burst from my chest.

Bending his head, Vale continued his ministrations, moving down lower… and lower.

Now that I was tied up, I could sense my whole body reacting with small shivers of anticipation. Every touch of Vale's hand made my skin jump. The air was getting chilly, but I was burning inside.

"Jessica?"

"Take me."

I couldn't stand it anymore. I needed him. Vale bent down, but instead of taking off his clothes, he slid between my legs. A small cry escaped my lips as he parted my thighs with his strong hands. *Oh, Lord.*

He pinned down my hips against the thin padding, and let out a single breath across me. I shivered, my nerves shooting out pinpricks of desire in every direction. His mouth was only an inch away from my slick folds, only an inch away and yet it seemed so far.

I couldn't take it, I couldn't. I arched up, and felt his hands press harder to pin me down. My wrists tugged uselessly at the rope holding my arms taut above my head. And an agonizing bolt of desire wrenched through my body.

The sky was dark now, and when I looked over at him, the lantern shining from behind him gave him a golden halo of hair. His face was in shadow, but I could tell somehow that he was smiling.

All the fear was gone, replaced by an intense desire. I needed his touch, and a small moan left my lips as he stroked his hands around the outside of my legs, coming back to pin me again. He bent down and licked between my thighs. One slow, hard lick, enough to send a spasm running from my core down to my toes and up through my fingers.

I moaned.

"Did you enjoy that?" His voice was smiling. Every particle of my being strained forward to meet him. I needed more.

"Vale?"

"Yes?"

"Take me."

It was an order that I knew he would disobey, and while I loved him for tantalizing me, for stretching out the pleasure, there was also a thrill that came from telling him that I was his. I needed him to take me, needed to beg him for it, and the begging was part of the pleasure.

His tongue sliced down again, this time pressing against me more firmly. I gasped, drawing a breath of salty ocean air. My head tilted back and I saw only the bright pinpoints of the stars above, emerging from the darkening sky.

"Please," I moaned. "Oh please, *please.*"

"Jessica, I want you to be ready for this."

My whole body was pinned down, and as his tongue slid over me again and again, I found that he was matching the rhythm of the sea. As the ocean swelled under the boat, we rocked back and forth slightly. And with every rock, his tongue slid deeper and deeper into me.

My legs pinned together, wrapping tightly around his body, urging him to do more. I needed more—more pressure. I couldn't bear how gentle he was.

"Now?" he asked. The question itself was a tease. I whipped my head sideways to look at him.

"I'm yours."

It was enough. It was all that he needed. He tore the clothes from his body, and I saw him in silhouette as he undressed. His muscles were broad planes stretched taut beneath his skin, the light shining over the crisp edges. He knelt down again between my legs, his strong thighs parting mine. I'd drawn them together, but now I unraveled easily at his touch. He could do anything to me, as long as he gave me what I was here for.

As though reading my thoughts, he smiled. I could see only the dim edge of the curve of his lips, inches away from mine. His fingers threaded through my hair, then cupped the back of my head. He lifted me up slightly, and as his lips met mine, I felt him slide into me.

It was a sensation unlike anything I'd ever felt before. His cock was so thick, so *hard*. I hadn't imagined the way my body would mold to him, clenching tighter as he pushed into me. For one unimaginably wonderful second, I didn't breathe. I didn't need to. This was all I needed— his body and mine, now together.

Then he shifted slightly, pulling out of me, and the

hollow ache I felt sent a growl through my throat. I wanted to speak but couldn't.

Don't stop.

The insistent desire beating through my body made me arch my hips up to meet him. A sharp pain shocked me as he thrust forward, but then the pain was overshadowed by the thrills of pleasure as my body clenched around his thick cock.

"Jess—"

"*Yes,*" I gasped.

Yes. This was what I'd wanted. This—the tug of rope on my wrist, the pressure of his hands on my hips, and now his cock deep inside me, filling me in a way I'd never thought possible.

He rocked forward, and I shuddered. A deeper pleasure was working its way through me. It was a dark, terrible need that was only beginning to be satisfied. I felt him rock out, slick between my legs, and then thrust in deeper. I cried out, helpless beneath him to do anything but scrape the air for my next breath. The waves shattered on the side of the hull, and I gripped the rope that held my wrists together, trying not to shatter myself.

The coil inside my body tightened, tightened like a spring wound beyond its breaking point. He rocked into me and I rocked back, until we were both waves on the ocean's surface and there was nothing between our bodies. I was his, his completely.

Most of the time when I'd touched myself, it was with my eyes closed. This time, though, I kept them open, even though it was dark outside. I wanted to see everything, remember everything. The sound of the waves under us, and the smell of salt in Vale's hair as he buried his head into the crook of my neck. The slick friction as he thrust in slowly, then out, so gentle and yet so insistent.

Above us, the stars were pinpoints in the dark sky, and his features were in shadow, but it was him right there with me, him that I wanted.

He began to rock faster and faster, his cock impossibly hard inside of me. His rhythm arched me up with every thrust, and I wrapped my legs tight around him, meeting his body with mine, like two waves crashing together to become one.

The coil grew even tighter in my core, and I could feel the waves starting to crest inside.

"Ohhh."

His moan thrilled me, shook me deeply. He wasn't in control, and neither was I. There was something between us that was wrapped all around our bodies, that had taken us over entirely. Every nerve that fired, every breath I gasped, was something more than just me alone. I wanted him, and he wanted me, and our desire was like a living, breathing creature that roared out of control.

When my orgasm came, it was deeper than any climax I'd ever had. I felt the shudder start in my core and ripple outwards.

"Oh!" I cried soundlessly. My hands grasped at the taut rope for balance. His cock stiffened inside of me, and the waves crashed through my body. I screamed aloud, and the sound seemed impossibly loud in the middle of the ocean, here where nobody would hear.

"Yes! Yes!"

I arched up, wanting every inch of my body to be covered by his, and he spasmed, his thick cock thrusting even deeper into me as he was taken over by his own orgasm. I could feel his shudders against me and it made me come again and again, shaking uncontrollably with pleasure.

"*Ohhhhh!*"

He groaned, a brute animal noise, as his hands clasped my body. He held me for a moment more before I felt him withdraw. An animal sound choked my throat as he withdrew, and I bit back on it.

I shivered as he collapsed next to me, his arms trembling. In that moment, I thought I could hear his heartbeat, the same way I'd heard it in the cell. It was only when he dropped back onto his side, away from me, that I realized it was my own pounding heart.

I couldn't say anything. What I'd been so scared of, the act I'd thought would hurt, always, had turned out to be something wonderful and beautiful. His body meeting mine in pure need. Giving myself to him entirely as he gave himself to me.

The air was cold, and growing colder. Shivers of pleasure made my arms prickle, and I nuzzled against his side.

With one arm, he reached up and deftly untied the knot holding my wrists. I brought them down, noticing that my hands were shaking. Vale clasped both of my hands in his broad palm, his fingers curling around mine. He kissed my forehead, and I found that I was crying with happiness.

"I love you," he said simply.

Dizzy with pleasure, I looked up into ice-blue eyes marked with concern. I smiled, then laughed aloud. My laughter carried over the open water.

"I love you, too."

We lay there, our naked bodies pressed together, and all around us the swells of the ocean lifted the boat and pressed against the hulls in small splashes. A perfect contentment filled me.

"Did you want to go inside?" Vale whispered. "It's starting to get cold."

His fingers stroked my hair and I nuzzled into his chest. His body was warm, his arms comforting, and the sky was infinite above our heads.

"Just a bit longer," I said, and closed my eyes.

The End

Thank you for reading Yours!

If you enjoyed the story would you please consider leaving a review on Amazon?

Just a few words and some stars really does help!

-

Be sure to sign up for my mailing list to find out about new releases, deals and giveaways!

http://bit.ly/AubreyDarkNewsletter

Made in the USA
Middletown, DE
26 September 2015